BLUDGEONING AT THE BOUTIQUE

KELLY HASHWAY

CONTENTS

To Ayla with love

CHAPTER ONE

Third times a charm. That's what I'm telling myself anyway as I pull into the parking lot of Belle Boutique, which is where the Traum Temp Agency sent me. This is my third job placement since moving to Rockland, and to say my last two were less than stellar is a gross exaggeration. I'm starting to think I'm a magnet for dead bodies since I have a knack for finding them—so far at each of my places of employment.

I pull into a parking spot only to see Ben Traum's Silverado parked near the door. Ben is technically my boss since it's his temp agency that I work with. Well, his and his father's. Not that Lukas Traum does much work these days. He sort of handed the business over to Ben so Ben would be forced to choose a career. That's something I can relate to since I spent countless years in college studying everything under the sun and coming out with no degree in anything. Hence, I work with a temp agency. So Ben and I have a lot in common, which is why we're quickly becoming good friends. Or friends who like each other as more than friends but are also afraid of ruining the friendship. It's a little complicated.

I get out of my car and smile at him as he meets me at my door. "I wasn't expecting to see you here."

He awkwardly clasps his hands in front of him. "I wanted to wish you luck on your first day."

"How did you know I'd be twenty minutes early?" I ask, dipping my head at him.

He bobs one shoulder. "Lucky guess."

Movement out of the corner of my eye draws my attention to a man picking up trash. "Pete!" I exclaim, rushing over to him. Pete Modell is one of my favorite residents in Rockland. He's had a lot of bad luck in his life, including being involved in an accidental homicide and also losing his business. But he's the most caring person and knows everyone in town to the point where I'd bet he's considered practically family by most of the people who live here.

"Hailey Hart," Pete says, "it's good to see your smiling face."

"I'm so happy to see you back in town. I wasn't sure how long you'd be away."

"Community service is good for the soul. I admit I stayed longer than I'd intended, but we were doing good work. I even got to help build houses for the less fortunate." Pete smiles. I get the feeling he's the type of person who truly believes everything happens for a reason.

"It's great to have you back, Pete," Ben says.

Pete tugs down on the rim of his baseball cap. "I'm guessing you got yourself a new job here at the boutique, Hailey."

"I did. It's my first day."

"Well then, a word of advice. Look out for Simone. She's not the nicest woman. Her brother Laurent is much more personable."

Simone and Laurent Vincent are co-owners of the boutique. They also happen to be brother and sister. Laurent is the one I spoke with on the phone, so I've yet to have an encounter of any kind with Simone.

"I appreciate the heads-up." I jerk a thumb at Ben. "This one here conveniently left out that piece of information."

Ben holds up both hands. "I've never had any trouble with Simone."

Ben's a very attractive guy in his late twenties. I doubt he has trouble with many women.

"I'm sure you'll be fine," Pete says. "You're easy to like, Hailey."

"Thank you, Pete. And welcome home."

"Spoken like a true Rockland native. We are quickly making you one of us." He dips his hat to Ben and me and walks away to continue cleaning up the streets.

"I guess I should get inside," I tell Ben.

"Can I take you to dinner to celebrate your first day on the new job? I promise there won't be seafood."

Ben accidentally planned our first "maybe a date" at a seafood place. Seafood is the only food I don't eat.

"I'm in. Call me later." I gently squeeze his arm before walking toward the back door of the boutique.

As soon as I approach, I hear voices. Or more like yelling. A woman is clearly upset, and I'm getting a very distinct feeling I'm about to meet the infamous Simone Vincent. I pause, not sure if I should knock since there's clearly an argument in progress on the other side of the door. I'm not certain they'd hear me knock over the yelling, though, so I open the door and step into a storage room.

The woman stops screaming and glares at me, but the man smiles and walks over to me. "You must be Hailey, yes?"

I nod. "Yes, sir."

"Please, call me Laurent. None of this *sir* business. This is my sister, Simone. We are so happy to have you join us here at Belle Boutique."

"I'm very happy to be here."

"Yes, well, we'll see about that. The last girl was a nightmare," Simone says. "You get two days to impress me, or I'll be calling that temp agency and requesting someone else."

"I'm a hard worker. Just let me know what you'd like me to do, and I'm sure I can perform the job to your liking." I really want to tell her I suspect the last girl quit because Simone is so nasty, but Laurent seems nice, so I restrain myself for his benefit.

"Have Charlene show her around." Simone flips her hand in the air.

"Charlene quit four months ago," Laurent says. "Hailey, you'll shadow Leslie today."

"Sounds great." I follow Laurent from the back room.

"This is my office here." Laurent points to a door. "You're welcome to come see me anytime." He gives me a warm smile. "This is Simone's office over here." He pauses. "Come see me before interrupting her. She deals mostly with the designers whose products we sell here. I handle the employees."

I bob my head.

"And here is the store itself." He brings me into the large open room. One wall is just shelves filled with designer handbags. Another wall is all shoes. And the center of the store is full of designer clothing on racks and mannequins. "That curtain over there is the dressing room. We only have one, so it's unisex," Laurent says. "Your job will mainly be making sure the store looks in tiptop shape. Everything on the shelves needs to be neat and perfectly folded, which means tending to it after customers browse."

"No problem," I say.

"Leslie will handle the registers. I'm aware you have experience using a register, so we might train you for that later if need be." He's making it sound like he plans to keep me around, despite Simone's threat of canning me in two days if she isn't impressed with me.

"I'm happy to do whatever you need," I say.

"Good. We like to keep the stock full, so anytime a customer makes a purchase, you'll need to look for the item in the back storage room and bring out a replacement."

"Got it."

"Sometimes, customers will put in orders for different sizes of items as well. There are forms to fill out behind the counter for that. Leslie will help you with those."

I look around, wondering where this Leslie woman is. According to the clock on the wall, we're supposed to be opening in a matter of minutes. "What time does Leslie get in?" I ask.

"Oh, she's here. I'm sure she's in Simone's office, making her morning coffee."

How is making Simone's coffee in Leslie's job description? She's not a personal assistant.

Laurent looks at me and laughs. "No, Hailey, you won't be asked to make coffee. Leslie took that upon herself. She was never asked to do it, but it's become sort of a routine by this point."

I wonder if Leslie felt she needed to get on Simone's good side to keep her job.

"Ah, there she is." Laurent extends a hand. "Good morning, Leslie."

"Bonjour, Monsieur Vincent." Leslie looks at me. "You must be Hailey."

"Yes, nice to meet you." I extend my hand, which she shakes.

"Hailey, I leave you in very capable hands," Laurent says. "I'll be in my office if anyone needs anything."

"Thank you," I call after him.

"Laurent's a sweetheart," Leslie says. "It's Simone you need to worry about sucking up to."

I turn to face her. "Is that why you make her coffee in the mornings?"

"Laurent told you about that?" She nods. "Yeah, I find her easier to deal with when she's caffeinated, so it serves two purposes."

I don't have the heart to tell Leslie that Simone doesn't even know her name. "Simone mentioned a Charlene that used to work here."

"Oh, yeah, she quit about four months ago. She didn't last long at all."

"How long have you been here?" I ask.

"Two years now. I started right out of college. I want to go into design, but it's a tough business. I got the job here the summer after I graduated. It was only supposed to be temporary, but I like working with the designers, and Laurent's really great, too. So I'm still here. How about you? What brought you here?"

It's the question I hate answering. I moved to Rockland so no one would know I wasted my life savings on a college education in everything and nothing at the same time. "I'm new in town."

"Wait. Are you *that* new girl?"

"I'm not sure what you mean."

"The one I read about in the Rumor Robin column."

Rumor Robin is a gossip column in the *Rockland Record*. The author of the column happens to be my best friend, Riley Jacobs, except I'm the only one in town who knows that other than Riley and her boss, who also happens to be her uncle.

"Yeah, that would be me, unfortunately."

"Why unfortunately? You're like a super sleuth or something. I think it's pretty cool."

That column ran after I solved my first murder in Rockland. Riley spun it to sound like I solved the case before the police could. What really happened was more like luck, but Riley likes to stick it to Detective Garrett Bilson any chance she gets. She and Garrett have this elementary school crush going on where they pretend to not like each other even though I'm pretty sure they both are secretly in love with the other.

"I'm hoping this job will be less eventful," I say.

Leslie unlocks the front door. "It's not that busy on weekdays. We get the stay-at-home moms mostly. Lunchtime is the busiest because people stop in on their lunch breaks."

"So when do we take ours?" I ask.

"Early or late," she says. "I usually take the one o'clock to one thirty, so you can either take eleven to eleven thirty or one thirty to two."

"Do I have to decide now?"

"Not at all. You can let your stomach decide each day if you'd like. If you're hungry that morning, take the earlier lunch. If you're not hungry, take the later. It's pretty flexible."

"Great. Does anyone else work here?" I ask, straightening a pile of satin shirts.

"Just Jesse, but he's still in high school, so he doesn't get here until almost three o'clock."

"Doesn't the boutique close at six most days?"

"Yeah, he works weekends, too, which is nice because it means I can take days off when I need." She's making it sound like she usually works seven days a week.

A man opens the door of the boutique. Judging by the expression on his very red face, he's not happy. "Where's Simone?" he asks, not making eye contact with Leslie or me.

"Ms. Vincent is in a meeting, Mr. Sinclair. I could have her call you when she's free," Leslie says.

"I need to see her now." He starts for the back of the store, but I step in his path.

"You can't go barging into her office," I say.

"I'm getting Laurent," Leslie says, hurrying past me. "Keep him there," she tells me, as if I can stop this man.

"Who are you anyway?" Mr. Sinclair asks me.

"Hailey Hart. I'm new here."

"I suggest you put in your notice. You don't want to work for someone like Simone Vincent. She thinks she's better than everyone." Mr. Sinclair throws out his hand, gesturing to the back offices. "I know she's not really in a meeting. That's what they tell me every time I come here. Simone is just too full of herself to be bothered with talking to me."

Laurent comes walking into the room. "Mr. Sinclair, my sister had to step out for a moment. Won't you come to my office? I'd be happy to assist you."

Mr. Sinclair shakes his head, clearly not buying the story, but he follows Laurent all the same.

The rest of my morning is pretty uneventful. I help a few customers who are browsing. Mostly I'm just tidying up the store. I do have to check the back for different sizes of a few dresses and tops, though. I wind up working through my lunch break since Riley texts me to say she has to take her cat, Marley, to the vet for his checkup. I still don't know that many people in town, and going to lunch by myself seems sad.

Simone actually notices I don't take a lunch, and for the briefest of seconds, she looks at me without a scowl before she heads back to her office.

"I think she likes you," Leslie says.

I laugh. "I think she keeps coming out here in the hopes of finding a reason to fire me."

"Probably, but she's definitely impressed with your work ethic. That's the happiest I've seen her in the past two years."

A woman in her fifties with blonde hair walks in. I go over to help her, but Leslie stops me. "Good afternoon, Cynthia."

Cynthia holds up a piece of paper. "If you saw this check, you wouldn't be saying that. Where is Simone? She's seriously undercharging for my designer handbags."

I expect Leslie to give this woman the same excuse she gave Mr. Sinclair earlier, but instead, she says, "I believe she's in her office if you'd like to go back there."

Cynthia storms past us without another word.

I look at Leslie for an explanation. "Designers Simone works with are like employees. They can go see her when they stop by."

"So that Sinclair guy isn't a designer?" I ask.

"No, he wants to be, but Simone turned him down. He's been harassing her ever since. That's why Laurent and I intervened."

"Who are the designers Simone works with?" I should know in case Leslie is ever at lunch or in the bathroom when one comes into the shop.

"There's Cynthia Lynch, whom you just met, and Ruby Redford. Ruby provides most of the designs you see in the store."

"Ruby Redford sounds like a Hollywood stage name or something."

"Well, it is in a way. Her real name is Rebecca Redford, but she changed it for the fashion world. All her designs have the Ruby logo on them. She's making quite the name for herself that way."

Yet she sells her work here in the small town of Rockland? That can't be helping very much to establish her name.

The rest of my day passes in sort of a blur. Jesse shows up after school. He's nice enough. I can tell he wants to go into fashion after high school. He acts like this is his dream job. It almost makes me feel guilty for not appreciating the merchandise the way he does.

Right around six o'clock, my stomach growls loudly. I'm happy to be leaving soon and finally getting some food in my stomach.

A woman with red hair walks in wearing the tallest heels I've ever seen.

"Ms. Redford," Leslie says, "are you here to see Simone?"

"Yes, is she in?"

"She should be in her office," Jesse says. "Would you like me to escort you?" He offers her his elbow.

"Thank you." Ruby takes Jesse's arm, and they walk toward the back office.

"You can head out," Leslie tells me. "I just have to count the register, but you're free to go."

"Thanks. See you tomorrow." I walk to the storage room in back, but I only get two steps into the room when I scream. There in the middle of the room is Simone Vincent, lying facedown in a pool of her own blood, the back of her head bashed in.

And standing over her is a delivery man, holding a bloody metal clothing rack.

CHAPTER TWO

I don't even realize I'm screaming until everyone comes running to see what's the matter. Laurent pulls me back and rushes to his sister's side. "Call 911," he says.

Leslie whips out her phone and dials, and I'm thankful because I can't move. I'm not even sure I'm breathing.

Jesse and Ruby are standing behind me, watching as Laurent tries to find a pulse on Simone.

"I swear I found her like this," the delivery guy says.

"Why are you holding the murder weapon?" I ask, my voice sounding foreign to me.

"It was on top of her. I saw it and just reacted. I was only trying to see if she was okay." He puts the clothing rack down. It's one of those single bar racks that's easy to pick up. It appears it's also easy to bash someone's skull in with one as well.

"The police are on the way," Leslie says.

The police station is basically around the corner, so I'm sure Detective Bilson will be here in a matter of minutes. I can hear the sirens already.

I'm in a state of shock. Three jobs and three dead bodies. How does this keep happening to me? Without thinking, I dial Riley.

"Hey, do you have dinner plans?" she asks.

"Simone Vincent is dead," I say. "Detective Bilson is on his way."

She gasps into the phone. "I'll be right there."

I pocket my phone as Detective Bilson walks into the boutique behind me. I turn around and wave him over.

The look he gives me can only be described as "How do you always manage to find dead bodies?" Boy, do I wish I knew the answer to that question.

Laurent stands up, his hands bloody from touching the body. "I can't find a pulse."

"Mr. Vincent, please step back." Detective Bilson bends down next to Simone, but he doesn't even bother checking for a pulse. "Who found her?"

I raise my hand, but the delivery guy says, "I did."

"What's your name?" Detective Bilson asks, standing up and grabbing his notepad and pen from his pocket.

"Maxwell Decker. I was delivering a package, and I found her on the floor under that rack there." He points to the bloody metal rack. "I took it off of her to try to help, but it was too late."

"You touched the murder weapon?" Detective Bilson asks.

"I wasn't thinking. I just wanted to help her."

"What were you doing back here to begin with?" Detective Bilson asks.

"Deliveries are brought in the back," Laurent says. "Simone never wanted them coming through the store itself. She thought it was offensive to the customers."

"That's right," Maxwell says. "There were instructions to come in the back door. I even have the keycode for the back door."

"We change it at night to avoid break-ins, and change it back during the day to accommodate the deliveries." Laurent takes a deep breath, and I can tell he's having a hard time keeping it together.

More police officers and the CSI team show up.

"I'm going to need everyone to follow me into the shop area," Detective Bilson says. "I have a lot of questions to ask each of you. I'll start with you, Maxwell."

"You can use my office for the questioning. You'll be more comfortable in there," Laurent says. "The rest of us can wait in the boutique."

"Thank you." Detective Bilson motions for us to clear the area so the CSI team can get to work.

Riley walks in just as I'm entering the boutique. She rushes over and hugs me. "Are you okay?"

"I'm fine."

"Where's Garrett?"

"Questioning the delivery man in Laurent's office."

"Why the delivery man?" she asks.

"I found him standing over the body and holding the murder weapon."

"Oh." She sighs. "Well, at least this case should be easy for Garrett to solve."

"Maxwell says he found Simone and took the clothing rack off of her."

"Maxwell? You're not talking about Maxwell Decker, are you?"

"Yeah, why?"

"I know him. He's good friends with Pete Modell." She takes her phone from her pocket. "I need to call Pete. He should know about this."

I'm not sure Pete wants to get wrapped up in another murder investigation, but I suppose I'd want to know if one of my friends was being accused of killing someone.

Detective Bilson talks to Maxwell for a while. I'm sure he's grilling him over and over, trying to get Maxwell to mess up and say something incriminating.

"I wish I knew what was going on in that office," Riley says.

"I don't know what's taking so long," Ruby Redford says. I'd almost forgotten the designer was here. "The man was caught red-handed. Why are the rest of us even here?"

Detective Bilson finally emerges, and he has Maxwell in handcuffs. "I'm going to need statements from everyone here, but seeing as I'm bringing Mr. Decker in for the murder, I'm releasing you all for the evening. Expect to hear from me in the morning. I'll be questioning each of you." His eyes land on Riley. "What are you doing here?"

"Shopping," she says without missing a beat. She grabs a dress off the rack next to her. "Do you think I'd look good in this."

Detective Bilson's face turns red, but I don't think it's anger causing it this time. The dress Riley is holding up leaves little to the imagination.

"Riley, put that back." I take the dress from her and return it to the rack.

"Hailey, I'd like you to follow me to the station," Detective Bilson says. "Since you found Mr. Decker with the body, I really want to talk to you right away."

I nod because I figured as much.

"I'm coming with you," Riley says.

I had no doubt she would. We follow Detective Bilson out the front entrance since the police now have the back storage room roped off with police tape. It's going to be off-limits until this investigation is closed. I'm unfortunately all too familiar with how this works.

We walk around back to my Accord, which I've lovingly named Jane Honda. The old girl has over two hundred thousand miles on her, but she's still running, and I can't afford a new car. We drive to the station, and my phone rings on the way.

Riley answers the call on speaker for me. "Hey, Ben."

"Um, hello, Riley. I wasn't expecting you."

"Hailey's driving. To the police station, I might add."

"What happened?" Ben asks.

"One guess," I say.

"You've got to be kidding me."

"I really wish I was. It was Simone Vincent. I found the delivery man standing over her with the murder weapon."

"Well, at least it's an open and shut case," Ben says.

"Maybe not," Riley says. "The delivery guy is Maxwell Decker."

"Pete's friend?" Ben asks.

"That's the one." Riley shakes her head. "I don't think he's capable of murder."

I pull into a parking spot in front of the police station. "Ben, we're at the station now. I have to give a statement. Can I call you when we're finished?"

"Of course, but how about I bring dinner to your place? I have a feeling you won't be feeling up to going out after all this."

He knows me well. I'm not up for going out, and the only food in my apartment is cereal, peanut butter, and bread. "I'd like that. Thanks."

"Good luck," he says before hanging up.

Riley and I enter the police station and head directly for Detective Bilson's desk. He's not there, probably because he's busy booking Maxwell Decker. We sit and wait.

Pete Modell comes into the station and looks all around. Riley waves him over to us.

"What are you two doing here?" he asks us.

"I have to give a statement," I say.

"Hailey, I know Max. He didn't do this. He wouldn't." Pete grabs my hands. "Please. You're good at this sort of stuff. Please help him."

Pete's helped me time and time again. He saved me from being attacked more than once. I owe him this much.

"I'll do everything I can," I tell him.

Pete bobs his head and then wipes a tear from his eye.

Detective Bilson finally returns to his desk. "Well, this is a bigger crowd than I was expecting." He sits down and adjusts his tie.

"Why are you wearing that stupid thing?" Riley asks him. "It's not even tied correctly." She leans over the desk to fix it for him, which makes his cheeks redden again.

"Pete, I know Maxwell is a friend of yours, but he was literally caught with the murder weapon and the body. You understand I'm only doing my job here."

"Detective, I know it looks bad, but Max didn't kill Simone. He had no reason to." Pete places a hand flat on Detective Bilson's desk. "All he's guilty of is trying to help a woman."

"Motive is a necessary component to murder, Detective," I say. I've recently become addicted to true crime shows on TV. I watch them every night, despite my claims of trying to cut back. I just can't seem to help myself.

Detective Bilson glares at me. "Hailey, tell me exactly what happened when you found Simone Vincent's body."

"I was leaving for the day, and my car was parked around back, so I was planning to go through the storage room to the back door. I only made it about two steps into the room when I saw the body on the ground."

"Where was Maxwell Decker?"

I hate having to answer this with Pete standing next to me. I shift uncomfortably in my chair. "He was standing over the body."

Detective Bilson motions with his hand for me to continue.

"And he was holding the metal clothing rack."

"Did you see the blood on it?"

I swallow hard. "Yes."

"What did you do then?" Detective Bilson asks.

"I screamed."

"Like any sane person would," Riley says.

"My scream alerted everyone else, and they came running. Leslie called 911 while Laurent checked on Simone."

"Where was Mr. Decker when all that was happening?" Detective Bilson asks.

"He was standing there in shock. He said he found Simone on the floor with the metal rack on top of her. He moved it to try to help her, but he realized she couldn't be saved."

"See," Pete says. "Max was trying to help. He didn't hurt her."

Detective Bilson looks at Pete and then me. "Unfortunately, there's nothing to prove that's true. However, Mr. Decker's fingerprints are on the murder weapon, and he was found with the body. All the evidence points to him being the killer."

"Okay, let's say he had means and opportunity. Where's his motive?" I ask. "You still haven't answered that."

Detective Bilson rubs his forehead. "Hailey, I will look into that." He stares me directly in the eyes. "Did you hear me? *I* will. Not you."

"Can I talk to Max?" Pete asks.

"I'm afraid not," Detective Bilson says.

"Oh, come on, Garrett." Riley shakes her head. "Just let him talk to the man. What's it going to hurt?"

"Riley, could I have a word with you?" Detective Bilson stands up.

Riley rolls her eyes, but she follows him over by the water cooler.

"Do you think they'll ever admit their feelings for each other?" Pete asks me.

"Your guess is as good as mine."

Riley's arms flail out at her sides, and while I can't hear what either of them is saying, I'm pretty sure Riley is laying into him hard. A moment later, she walks back over to us with a smile on her face.

Detective Bilson says, "Follow me. All of you."

I look at Riley, but she just continues to smile.

Detective Bilson brings us to an interrogation room. "Sit. I'll be right back." He closes the door behind us.

"What's going on?" I ask Riley.

"He's getting Maxwell for us."

"Thank you, Riley," Pete says.

"I figured it's best if we all talk to him since I doubt Garrett will actually listen to what Maxwell has to say."

"You really are the best," I tell her.

"I know."

When Detective Bilson returns with Maxwell, he closes the door behind us and disables the camera in the room. "You have five minutes," he tells us.

"Tell us what happened," Pete says.

Maxwell lets out a long breath. "I was bringing in a package. At first, I didn't see the body because I was busy scanning the label on the package to mark it as delivered. I always announce myself when I enter a building, though, so I said my usual, "Delivery for Simone Vincent," and when no one answered me, I looked up. That's when I saw her." He pauses and looks down at his hands cuffed in his lap. "I thought maybe she'd fallen because the rack was on top of her, so I rushed over to help her. But when I got closer, I knew it was bad. There was so much blood, and that wound on the back of her head… I didn't think anyone could survive that."

They couldn't. Whoever killed Simone Vincent made sure she was dead before they left.

"Did you see anyone near the storage room?" I ask.

"No, but like I said, I wasn't looking up when I came into the building. Someone could have been in there, and I missed them by the time I finished scanning the package."

Pete's face pales. "If the killer was there and saw Max, he or she might not know that Max didn't see them. Max could be in danger."

He's not wrong. I look at Detective Bilson. "You have to protect him until we find the real killer."

Detective Bilson sighs. "As of right now, I'm convinced I have the killer in custody already. I'm taking Mr. Decker back to his holding cell." He motions for Maxwell to stand. "Let's go. Your time's up."

Riley starts to protest, but I grab her arm to stop her. We watch Maxwell and Detective Bilson walk out.

"Hailey, please," Pete says.

"Pete, believe me; I have no intention of letting Maxwell take the blame for this. But if you're right about the killer seeing Max, then he's in danger. The best thing for him is to be in that holding cell under police protection while we catch the real killer."

CHAPTER THREE

Ben and I finish eating the Italian food he brought over while a true crime show plays on the TV in the background.

"I'm going to find you a new job placement," he says.

"No." I shake my head. "With my track record, I'd show up there and find a body on my first day, too. I can only handle one investigation at a time."

"I wish I could laugh like that was a joke, but I'm afraid it might actually be true." He leans back on the arm of the couch. "I'm so sorry, Hailey."

"It's not your fault."

He cocks his head at me. "They call my business the Traumatic Temp Agency for a reason. We're cursed. I might be trying to renovate the old building that houses our office, but the place is clearly haunted or something with the way all this bad stuff keeps following our employees."

Ben's been doing a major overhaul on the building, which really does look like a haunted house. The first time I saw it, I was afraid it was going to collapse with me inside. But the improvements he's making are really turning the place around. At least as far as appearance goes.

"Your business is not cursed. I might be, though."

He reaches for my hand. "Nothing like this happened to you before you started working with me. I take the full blame. I think I need to talk to my dad about closing the doors."

"What would you do?" Ben doesn't have aspirations to do anything else.

"I wish I knew."

"We're quite the pair," I say, squeezing his hand.

Without warning, he leans forward and kisses me. As soon as he pulls away, he says, "Sorry. I shouldn't have done that."

"I'm not sorry you did."

"Really?" He looks surprised.

"Really." I've liked Ben from the start, but murder investigations seemed to get in the way of us actually dating. Now I'm starting to think there may always be an investigation going on, so waiting until there isn't one might not be an option.

He smiles at me. "I should go. It's getting late, and you have work tomorrow."

"Yeah, lucky me. All these murders occur in back rooms so the stores can still stay open." The sarcasm in my voice is thick.

Ben laughs. "Well, it does mean you continue to get paychecks, so there's that."

"Yeah, I suppose you're right. I do need to keep making money." I stand up and walk him to the door. "Thank you for dinner and for coming over tonight to follow up about my job placement."

"You know that's not really why I come see you, right?"

"I do now," I say with a smile.

He leans down and kisses my cheek. "Good night, Hailey."

"Drive safely," I say before closing the door. Today ranks up there with some of the worst days of my life, but one good thing came from it. Ben and I finally admitted our feelings for each other. This could be the start of something really good.

Leslie lets me in the front door of the boutique since the back entrance isn't accessible. "Hey, I wasn't sure if you'd show up today."

"Really? I'm sort of the only one who's dealt with something like this before," I say, placing my purse behind the counter.

Leslie gives a nervous laugh. "Yeah, I guess you're right about that. How do you deal with it? I mean last night I had several nightmares about dead bodies popping up everywhere."

And I watched a true crime show to fall asleep. Am I weird for finding murder comforting and something to fall asleep to? Maybe I am in the wrong profession. Maybe I should have gone into law enforcement. Of course, I'm not sure I could work alongside Detective Bilson. I've had to do it here and there on the two cases I've investigated, and it was not fun by any means. I'm not sure I want to have to follow police protocol either. There are too many rules.

"Well, I heard the police are pretty positive they have the right man in custody." Since I don't know who killed Simone, I have to play along with the ruse that Maxwell Decker is the killer. It's the only way to keep him safe from the real killer. Not that I think Leslie is the killer. She and I were together almost the entire day. The only times she was out of my sight were when she took her lunch break and when she used the bathroom. I suppose it's possible she killed Simone during a bathroom break, but I'm not sure she could pull off murdering her boss and then going back to work as if nothing happened. I'm also pretty certain the bludgeoning would have caused some blood splatter.

Blood splatter! Maxwell Decker didn't have any blood splatter on him. But if I point that out to Detective Bilson and Maxwell is released, he'll be in danger if the killer really was still in the storage room when Maxwell arrived. I'm not sure what to do with this information, so I text Riley.

"Everything okay?" Leslie asks me, motioning to my phone. "Looks like a long message."

"Oh, yeah. I just forgot to check on my friend's cat." That is the worst coverup ever, but it was all that came to mind.

"Aw, is the poor kitty sick?" Leslie asks.

Thank goodness she's an animal lover.

"He had to go to the vet yesterday. I'm just making sure every-thing is okay with him."

"Animals are such amazing creatures, aren't they?"

I can't afford to have a pet, so I wouldn't really know. I didn't have any growing up either. I offer a weak, "Yeah," in response.

"I have two cats. They're brothers. They get into everything, but I love them." She finishes setting up the register for the day and then unlocks the front door. "Should we expect people to avoid the boutique out of fear or flock to it to find out what happened?"

"Most likely the latter. People are curious by nature."

"That's sort of what I figured. It's morbid, though."

Laurent comes from the back, which startles me because I'm pretty sure he's not supposed to be back there. "Hailey, I'm glad you're here. I was worried you'd quit."

"Are you allowed in your office?" I ask.

"Yes, only the storage room is off-limits."

"You were in your office yesterday when…" I can't bring myself to say "when the murder happened" because it was the man's sister who was killed.

"Yes, I was."

"And Leslie and I were here. Yet none of us heard anything. Not a scream or a struggle. How is that possible?"

Leslie holds up a finger. "Wait. Weren't Jesse and Ruby in Simone's office? Did anyone find out if Simone was with them at any point?"

Laurent and I exchange a look. Neither one of us thought to ask, but Leslie is making a good point.

"I just thought of something. If Simone didn't put up a fight of any nature, it means she was attacked from behind. So either someone snuck up on her, or she knew her killer and wasn't afraid to turn her back on the person."

"Wow, you really are good at this, Hailey," Leslie says.

"I don't know who she could have been with at the time," Laurent says. "She didn't have a meeting on her schedule. It was the first thing I checked after the police left."

"Who would want to harm her?" I ask.

Laurent looks down at his shoes, which no doubt cost more than my monthly rent. "Simone had a personality that most didn't understand."

"Or care for," Leslie adds.

Laurent bobs his head. "Yes, I suppose that is true."

Then plenty of people disliked her. Even Pete Modell warned me about her, so her reputation was well-known and not in a good way. "Are there cameras in the store?" I ask.

"Only in the actual boutique," Laurent says. He gently turns me to see the two cameras positioned on the ceiling.

Just once, I'd love for a murder to be on tape. Why is that so much to ask for?

Laurent studies my face. "You don't think the delivery man is the guilty party, do you, Hailey?"

"It doesn't really matter what I think. The police have to figure out if he's guilty or not." I don't believe that for a second, but I can't let anyone know I'm investigating on my own. No one other than Riley, Ben, and Pete that is.

Customers come into the store, two women, one with a stroller. Leslie and I spring into action, and Laurent excuses himself to his office again.

We have more customers than usual all morning, so I feel a little bad when eleven thirty rolls around and I tell Leslie I'm taking my lunch break. But, I am guaranteed a break, and since I didn't take one yesterday, I'm not passing up the opportunity today.

"It's fine. Go," she tells me. "I'll be taking my break later and leaving you to handle things here. Besides, Laurent is in his office if I need another hand." She waves me out of the store.

I only have thirty minutes, so I text Riley to meet me at the sandwich shop for a quick lunch and to discuss the case. She's already there when I get there. I swear she never works. Though most of what she does is eavesdrop on people in town to get material for her gossip columns, so she really does need to be out and about all the time.

"Interesting," Riley says as we eat. "If she knew her killer, it could be someone she's related to, friends with, or works with."

"Yes. You're thinking it's her husband, aren't you?"

"True crime tells you the spouse is always the prime suspect."

"Do you know him?" Riley knows everyone in town.

"Vance Brooks."

"Brooks?" How didn't I realize that Simone never took her husband's last name. It's the only explanation for her and Laurent having the same last name.

"Yeah, he was openly unhappy about her not changing her name, but Simone claimed she was too big in the fashion world to risk changing it."

"Too big? She has a tiny boutique in a small town. That's not big on any scale."

"Yeah, well, her ego was through the roof, and she thought very highly of herself in every aspect of her life."

"What was her relationship with her husband like? Did they fight a lot?"

"Simone loved to yell at people. Vance was no exception. She yelled at him every chance she got. I remember he bought her a new car for her birthday, and she yelled at him because she wanted this metallic blue color that the car didn't even come in. He got her black." Riley flips a hand in the air. "The horror."

"So why did he stay with her if she was so awful?"

"Beats me. I don't try to figure people out that way. She leans over the table toward me and whispers, "I did write about the car incident in the Rumor Robin column, though."

I'm not surprised in the least.

"Think we should talk to Vance and see if he had any reason to want to kill his wife?"

"Can't hurt. I mean as an employee, you could easily stop by his house to offer your condolences."

Yes, I could. "And I could easily need to use the bathroom after drinking too much and conveniently wind up in their bedroom by mistake."

Riley laughs. "Oh, if Garret could hear us now."

I check the time on my phone. "I have to get back to work. Meet me at the boutique at six when we close, and we'll go pay Mr. Brooks a visit."

"You absolutely will not do that."

I turn around to see Detective Bilson looking like he's ready to slap handcuffs on Riley and me.

CHAPTER FOUR

Riley shoos me, trying to get me out of the sandwich shop and away from Detective Bilson. "Don't be late. You'll get fired on your second day."

I back away toward the exit.

"Hailey," Detective Bilson says, "I mean it. Don't go anywhere near—"

I'm through the door and onto the street. I have to run to get back to work on time, but luckily it isn't far at all.

Leslie looks relieved when I step inside the boutique. Most of the shoppers are just pretending to browse. They're actually trying to get glimpses into the back rooms. It's going to be a long day if this keeps up. I move a rack in front of the doorway to the back area and drape several long scarves over it to create a makeshift curtain.

"Ooh, how lovely." A woman walks over, pretending to be interested in the scarves. She reaches for one—I'm sure to move it aside and see into the back area—but I step in between her and the scarves.

"There are more for you to look at on that table right there. This is just a display." I point to the table.

The woman scowls at me, but I cross my arms and stand my ground. Once she's moved on, I hurry to the register and grab a marker and paper from behind the counter. I write "Do NOT Touch" on the paper and then go hang it on the scarves I made the curtain out of.

Laurent nearly scares me half to death when he steps out from behind the scarves. He takes one look at the barrier I've created and bobs his head. "Good thinking, Hailey."

"Thank you."

"I have to run out for a little while. I'm afraid there is a lot to take care of now that my sister…" He lets the rest of his statement trail off.

"Of course. We'll be fine here." I don't want to believe Laurent would kill his sister to get full control of the business, but I can't deny it is a viable motive. He seems so nice, and from what I've seen, everyone likes him. Is that his true nature, though, or is he putting on an act? Simone wasn't exactly the caring type, and Laurent is her brother. It's possible they're more alike than different. Laurent just might be better at hiding his true colors than Simone was. Or Simone didn't even care to try.

Before I know it, it's time for Leslie's lunch break. "Good luck," she tells me before she heads out. Usually Laurent is here to work the register when Leslie takes her break, but he's still nowhere to be seen. And in all the commotion Leslie forgot to show me how to use the register. I'm going to have to wing it and hope for the best if any of these people actually purchase anything.

I keep myself positioned near the scarf curtain I made. My sign seems to be working because no one is actually touching the scarves, but they are still going near them and trying to peer around them. A few people aren't even attempting to be discreet about it, either.

After about twenty minutes on my own, I get fed up and make an announcement. "If you're only here because of the murder, please find your way to the exit. If you plan to buy something, you should be on line at the register." My tone isn't exactly friendly, and if Simone were alive, she'd fire me on the spot for talking to customers this way.

A few people walk out, giving me disapproving looks in the process.

"Have a nice day," I say, my tone not matching my words.

One woman does buy a scarf, and luckily, the register is easy enough to figure out. I ring up the sale and send her on her way as well. That's when I get a moment of peace. The shop is empty. I look up at the clock. I have only about three minutes before Leslie returns from her break, and Laurent is still gone as well. If I really want to find out if Laurent isn't the person he appears to be, I have to act quickly.

I hurry across the shop and through the scarves to Laurent's office. The door is closed but not locked. A guilty person would most likely lock it, but I'm not about to turn back now. I open the door and step inside, closing the door behind me.

Laurent's office is very neat, the exception being his desk. There are papers scattered all over it, which are a stark contrast to the perfectly lined books on the shelves, arranged in height order, and the impeccably trimmed bonsai trees on the windowsill. I step toward the desk to see what the papers are. Some are contracts with designers. I only know that because I recognize Ruby Redford's name. Other papers mention the lease for this boutique.

"Hailey?" Laurent's voice calls out from the front of the store.

I quickly rush out of the office and shut the door behind me. Then I duck into the bathroom. I wait until I hear Laurent step into the back hallway before I emerge. "Laurent, sorry about that. I needed a bathroom break, and I jumped on the opportunity when the shop cleared out."

"That's okay." He looks beyond me to his office. That's strange. Is he making sure his door is still closed? And why would he be worried if I was inside his office? What does he have to hide?

"Oh, I had to use the register. I'm pretty sure I did everything right, though." I start for the register to show him, and Leslie returns.

"Leslie, I'm glad you're back," Laurent says. "Can you please make sure Hailey rang up her sale correctly? I have to get back to something."

"Of course." She walks behind the counter and puts her purse on the shelf. "Let's see what we have here."

I show her what I did.

"Yes, you did it correctly. Good job, Hailey. I'm sorry I didn't think to show you how to use the register before I left."

"That's okay. Things were crazy here. I didn't think to ask you either."

"Was it like this in the other place you worked?" She must not know this is actually the third time I've been through something like this. She only heard about the candy shop murder because Rumor Robin wrote about it.

"Yeah, it can get crazy."

"You poor thing. You must think you're cursed."

Exactly.

Ben comes into the shop and immediately smiles when he sees me.

"Do you know him?" Leslie asks me, giving Ben the once-over.

"We're sort of unofficially dating."

"Forget what I said about being cursed then." Leslie is practically drooling now.

Ben walks over to me, and it's more than a little awkward because neither one of us knows how to greet the other. Do we hug, kiss, awkwardly wave? Ben opts to shove his hands into his pockets and say hello.

"How's your day been going?" I ask him.

"Probably a lot less eventful than yours."

"Hi," Leslie says, interrupting us.

"Sorry. Ben this is Leslie. Leslie, Ben."

Ben extends his hand to her. "Nice to meet you."

"You too. I can't believe I've never seen you around town before."

Leslie is fresh out of college, which only makes her five years younger than I am and six years younger than Ben, but she still seems like a college co-ed to me. I doubt she'd hang out at the same places Ben does. And considering these days Ben spends most of his time at either my place or Riley's, there's not much chance of Leslie and Ben meeting.

I've zoned out and missed their entire conversation, which couldn't have been long to begin with. Ben is staring at me. "I'm sorry, what?" I ask, thinking he must have said something to me.

He laughs. "I asked if you had plans this evening."

"Oh." I don't want to mention how Riley and I are going to see Vance Brooks after I leave work today. Leslie can't know about that because it might get back to Laurent that way.

Ben's face falls.

"I sort of do, but you're welcome to join us," I say, hoping Ben will pick up on the fact that the plans are secretive in nature and involve Riley since she's my partner in crime here.

"Great," he says, and I'm relieved he got my true meaning.

"I'll text you with the details," I tell him.

A few more customers come in, and Ben takes that as his cue to leave.

"He's gorgeous, Hailey," Leslie says. "How did you get lucky enough to find him?"

I'm still staring after Ben. It's possible I'm really falling for him. "I work with his temp agency."

"I thought the temp agency in town was run by some old guy."

Ben's father isn't old. He's in his fifties. He's only retiring to force Ben to take over the business. "Lukas Traum is Ben's father."

"Oh, that makes more sense. Is he attractive? I mean you might be able to get a glimpse of what Ben's future is going to look like. If he looks like his father, that is."

"Excuse me," a woman says, and I'm thankful for the interruption because I don't want to talk about whether or not my "sort of boyfriend's" father is attractive for an older man. "Do you know if you have this dress in a size six?" She holds up a red dress.

We can't go into the storage room to check for other sizes. "Unfortunately, what we have out on the floor is what's currently available, but we'd be happy to order the dress in a size six for you if you're not in a hurry," Leslie says. She might be young, but she's good at her job.

"Would it be in by a week from this Saturday?" the woman asks.

"I can call the designer to find out for you." Leslie waves the woman over to her.

Pete Modell comes into the boutique, and I walk over to meet him. "Hi, Pete. How is Maxwell holding up?"

"He's scared. I told him we're going to help him and being under police protection is the best thing for him right now, but

I'm not sure that's making it any easier for him to endure being behind bars."

"Riley, Ben, and I are going to talk to Simone's husband later today to find out who might have wanted Simone dead." If not her husband himself.

Pete nods. "I was on the other side of the street when the murder happened. I wish I had been over here and saw something." Pete has a knack for seeing most things that happen in town.

"We'll figure this out." I'm not sure I can keep that promise, but I do know I'll do everything in my power to try.

At six o'clock, Riley shows up to get me, and I text Ben to tell him where to meet us. Riley knows Vance Brooks's address because there isn't a person in town she doesn't at least know of. She spends her days researching all the residents and trying to dig up dirt on them. It's made her very handy to have around.

Vance's house is sitting on an enormous piece of property at the edge of town. "Are you sure this is his address?" I ask as I pull up the driveway, which is so long it might as well be called a road.

"Yup. It used to be a farm, but not much farming happens around here anymore. Vance bought up all the land, tore down the barn and farmhouse, and built this monstrosity." She points through the windshield at the three-story house that looks like it should be an inn or boarding school. I'm guessing it has more rooms than my old elementary school.

I park the car and am about to text Ben to see where he is when his truck pulls up behind me. We get out and walk to the front door together.

"I'm guessing they have a housekeeper, a cook, and maybe even a butler," Riley jokes. "This has to be old family money, right? I mean the boutique can't possibly be pulling in that much money."

"But if Simone married into a wealthy family, why would she insist on keeping her own last name?" I ask. "I think it makes more sense that she's the one who had all the money."

"Which gives Vance plenty of reason to kill her for it," Ben says.

"But they were married," Riley says. "He must have had access to the money already, so why bother to kill his wife?"

"Maybe she controlled the bank accounts," I say. "If she didn't change her name, it's possible she never put his name on the accounts. They could have separate accounts altogether."

"Which he'd only get access to after she died," Riley says, snapping her fingers.

"Let's see if we can find out for sure," Ben says, ringing the bell.

The woman who answers the door is decked out from head to toe in designer clothing. She's definitely not someone who works here. "Can I help you?" she asks.

"Hi, we're looking for Vance Brooks. Is he home?" I ask.

"Who are you?" Her gaze volleys between us.

"I'm Hailey Hart. I work at Belle Boutique. This is Riley Jacobs and Ben Traum."

"Hailey, yes. Laurent mentioned you. I'm Ivy, Laurent's wife." She extends her hand to me, and I shake it.

"It's nice to meet you, Mrs. Vincent."

"Vance isn't home from work yet. I'm just here trying to help him sort through some things."

"Is it okay if we come inside and wait for Mr. Brooks?" I ask.

She nods and opens the door for us.

The entryway in the house is enormous. The ceiling is so high I feel like I'm looking up into the clouds. There's a staircase just beyond the entranceway, and it looks like something straight out of a movie set.

"This house is very impressive," I say.

"Simone wouldn't have it any other way." Ivy closes the door behind us.

"I didn't get to know her well at all," I say. "Monday was actually my first day working at the boutique."

"Well, consider yourself fortunate." She seems to realize her slip immediately. "Please forgive me. That was an awful thing to say."

"I'm aware that Simone wasn't as well liked as Laurent is."

"That's an understatement. I can see you're a kind person, Hailey." She gestures toward the room on our right. "Please have a seat."

The room looks to be a library. There are shelves of books all along the walls and several comfy-looking couches and reading chairs.

"Can I offer you something to drink?"

"No, we're fine. Thank you," I say, taking a seat on one of the couches. Ben sits beside me, but Riley remains standing.

"Vance should be home any minute now."

"I imagine you've all been very busy making arrangements," I say. "Laurent had to leave the boutique for a while. I feel bad that he seems so overwhelmed right now. I wish there was something I could do to help."

"Yes, um, well, with the business in both their names, I'm sure there's a lot of paperwork for him to do."

"Did Simone have a will?" Riley asks.

"We're still looking for one. Vance claims she did have one, but no one seems to be able to find it."

That's odd. Wouldn't her lawyer have a copy of it? I'm sure someone like Simone Vincent had a lawyer to handle such things. "What about the lawyer?"

"He said she insisted on holding on to the will. She didn't want anyone to know of its contents until…" She lowers her head. "We've searched everywhere."

Is that why Laurent had all that paperwork on his desk? Was he going through all the files to try to find the will? I'm not sure Simone would have kept it at the boutique, though.

"If it were me, I'd keep it in a safe," Ben says.

"We've checked there," Ivy tells him. "It was the first place we looked, but apparently, Simone didn't want it anywhere Vance had access to."

I'm sure Simone never thought she'd die at her age, so she probably didn't think to tell anyone where the will was hidden. I give it some thought. I wish I knew more about her. It might help me figure this out.

"Did she have anything she kept with her at all times?" Riley asks.

The look of realization that washes over Ivy's face is fleeting, but I pick up on it.

"Would you excuse me for a moment?" Ivy rushes out of the library.

"I think you just gave her an idea, Riley." I stand up and go to the doorway to see which direction Ivy ran off in. She's hurrying up the stairs.

"Should we follow her?" Riley asks.

We can't go barging upstairs after her. She'd probably throw us out of the house. "No, let's wait to see what she does."

The front door opens, and a man walks into the house. It must be Vance Brooks. When he sees me, he pauses.

"Who are you?"

"I'm Hailey Hart. I work at Belle Boutique. Your sister-in-law let us in."

"Ivy's here?" He looks around the entryway.

"She went upstairs."

He hurries up the stairs without another word.

"What's going on?" Riley asks.

"I'm not sure, but he didn't seem happy that Ivy was upstairs," I say.

"He sounded pretty surprised when you told him she was even here," Ben adds.

"I agree." I can't help wondering if there was a lot of bad blood in this family.

Vance comes rushing back downstairs. "Ivy isn't upstairs." He looks at Riley and Ben. "There are more of you? How did you all get in here?"

"Like I said, Ivy let us in."

"Ivy isn't here. Haven't you been listening to me?" Vance pulls his phone from his pants pocket. "I'm calling the police. You people are trespassing on private property."

He has no idea there's a much bigger problem here. His sister-in-law most likely found Simone's will and took off with it. The question is why?

CHAPTER FIVE

If Vance Brooks calls the police on us for trespassing—which we did not—Detective Bilson will make our lives miserable. I can't let that happen. "Mr. Brooks, wait! Please. I'm telling you your sister-in-law was here. She let us in, and we were discussing your wife's will. Something Riley said made Ivy take off up the stairs. We had no idea she left because she didn't tell us."

"What did you say to her?" he asks Riley.

"I asked if Simone has anything she kept with her at all times because if she really wanted her will to remain a secret to everyone, she probably didn't let it out of her sight."

Vance furrows his brow in thought. "And Ivy ran upstairs after that?"

"Yes. I watched her."

He sits down on the second to last step of the staircase. "Simone wouldn't carry papers around. But she did carry a flash drive."

People still use those? "You think her will was electronic?"

"It's certainly possible," Vance says. "Simone was a very secretive person. She didn't like to have a paper trail."

Guilty people avoid leaving paper trails. What was Simone up to that she didn't want anyone else knowing about?

"Who exactly are you people?" Vance asks, seeming to come out of the mental fog he's been in.

"I work at the boutique, and these are my friends. We wanted to offer our condolences and also find out if you can think of anyone who would benefit from your wife's death."

"The police already caught the man responsible. It was that delivery man."

"Right," I say. I have to pretend I think Maxwell committed the murder, but maybe I can spin this as him not working alone. "But the delivery man had no motive. Unless the motive was he was being paid to kill Simone. Paid by the person who wanted her dead and benefitted from her murder."

"You think he was hired to kill my wife?"

"Don't you think that's a possibility?" I ask.

Vance rubs his forehead. "I need to call my sister-in-law and find out if she has Simone's flash drive."

"Were Simone's belongings returned to you?" I ask.

He bobs his head. "I put them upstairs."

Which is why Ivy ran up there. She went to claim the flash drive before Vance could find it.

"Mr. Brooks, why would your sister-in-law want Simone's will?"

He lets out a deep sigh. "Without the will, Laurent can make an argument for my wife's money. Their parents were quite wealthy and left them each a sizable sum when they died. Laurent put most of his money into the business. Simone was more conservative when it came to the business. Simone was a number cruncher. She was always trying to save a penny. Laurent could claim expenses she owed him."

That doesn't seem like the Laurent I know. But then again, he was acting weird when he thought I might have gone into his office. And then there's Ivy, who clearly wanted that will and took off in a hurry.

Vance stands up. "I need you people to leave. I have something to take care of." He shoos us out the door and closes it behind us.

"Anyone else thinking there's no love between the members of this family?" Riley asks.

"Oh, there's love. Love of money," I say.

The garage door opens, making me jump.

"I say we follow him, which means we need to get out of the driveway so he doesn't see us."

We rush to our cars and pull out as quickly as possible.

Once I'm back on the main road, I turn off my headlights and pull over on the side of the road. Ben does the same. We wait for Vance to drive away, and then we follow.

He drives clear across town to a much more modest home, though it's still quite nice.

"This must be where Laurent and Ivy live," I say.

"Yup." Riley peers through the windshield. "Laurent must have hated that Simone flaunted her money, while he spent his on the business."

"It's odd that Simone made a show of being wealthy, yet her husband said she was always worrying about money. Do you think she spent most of it?"

Riley shrugs. "Beats me."

I stop at the end of the driveway and watch Vance knock on the front door. Laurent doesn't look happy to see him, but he lets him inside the house. I cut the engine and get out of the car. I want to sneak up on the people inside the house to hear if they're arguing and possibly what about. Ben follows Riley and me.

The voices are muffled at the front of the house, so we walk around the side. We can hear them the best at the back of the house, probably because there are large French doors leading to the back patio.

"Where is it? You had no right to even be inside my home, Ivy!" Vance yells. "I should call the police on you right now."

"You wouldn't dare. Besides, you can't prove I was ever in your home today."

"Sure, I can. I have video cameras."

Boy, I really hope Laurent and Ivy don't, or we'll show up on them right now. Ben must be worrying about the same thing because he's looking up at the house, trying to locate any cameras. He shakes his head when he doesn't find any.

"Give me the flash drive. I know you found it," Vance says.

"I don't know what you're talking about." If I had to guess, I'd say Ivy probably has her arms crossed in front of her chest. I wish I could see them, but I don't want to risk them seeing me in return, so I'm staying off to the side of the doors and out of view.

"Those people told me you were there. I have eye witnesses. So unless you want me to go to the police, hand over the flash drive this instant." It certainly doesn't sound like an idle threat. Vance is ready to call the police right now.

"Ivy," Laurent says in a barely audible voice. Or at least it's barely audible through the doors.

"We don't even know what's on it," she says.

"That's for me to find out," Vance replies, and I'm assuming Ivy gave him the flash drive because the next thing I hear is the front door of the house slamming shut. He's leaving, which means he's going to see our cars parked out front. I have to hope he's angry enough with Ivy and Laurent that he doesn't tell them they have company.

We wait until we hear Vance's car pull away before we go back to our own vehicles.

"Let's go to my place," Riley says. "We need to talk this through."

We might also need to loop Detective Bilson in on what we've discovered if we plan to get any more information about what's on that flash drive.

Riley orders pizza from Dominic's on the way, and the delivery guy shows up the same time we get to her townhouse. She pays him and lets us inside. Marley, Riley's cat, comes to say hello briefly before returning to the couch to take a nap.

"I know all families have secrets, but those people seem really unusual to me," Ben says, grabbing bottles of water from Riley's refrigerator. We've all made ourselves very comfortable in each other's places. Well, all except for Ben's place. Riley and I still haven't been there. In fact, I don't even know where he lives.

"Ben, why have we never been to your place?" I ask as I get paper plates from the cabinet over the stove.

"You haven't told her?" Riley asks.

My gaze flits from Ben to Riley and back to Ben again. "Told me what?" Please don't say he lives with his ex or something crazy like that.

Ben sighs. "I live above the temp agency. There's an apartment upstairs."

That's why he's renovating the building. He lives there. And he's always at my place or Riley's because there's construction going on at his apartment. "You could have just told me that. It's nothing to be ashamed of."

"Come on, Hailey. You've seen the temp agency. Until I get my place renovated, too, I can't bring anyone there."

"I wouldn't care," I say. He has to know I don't put much value on having nice things. My apartment is a converted detached garage.

He moves toward me. "I know you wouldn't, but it bothers me. I don't want anyone to know I live there until I fix up the place and make it look respectable."

I can't fault him there because I was beyond embarrassed when he showed up at my apartment for the first time. Other than Ben and Hailey, the only person who knows where I live is Detective Bilson. I use a PO Box because I don't want to give anyone my address. Ben and I are more alike than I ever realized.

"Not that this little exchange isn't cute and all, but I'm starving, and you're holding my plate," Riley says, gesturing to the plates in my hand.

"Sorry," I say, bringing the plates to the table.

Ben gets us each a slice to start.

As we eat, I fill them in on Laurent's suspicious behavior today.

"If he's hurting for money, it's possible he killed Simone to try to claim those expenses she owed the business," Ben says.

"But what everyone forgets is that when someone dies, you aren't responsible for their debt," Riley says. "Companies like to make relatives think they are, but they're actually not."

"Yes, but if Simone and Laurent have a business account, which they must," I say, "then it's possible Laurent could pull money from there. Simone might have it set up to feed money into it from another one of her accounts."

"Laurent wouldn't be able to do that himself, though," Ben says. "He'd need Vance at this point, so then why did Ivy try to go behind Vance's back and steal the flash drive with the will on it?"

"Maybe she wanted to see if Simone left money to Laurent first," I suggest.

"We may never know what that will says." Riley wipes her mouth with a napkin. "Not without getting our hands on the flash drive."

Ben shakes his head. "We can't steal it."

"But if Vance misplaced the flash drive, and we happen to find it, look at what's on it, and then return it…" Riley bobs one shoulder. "I'm just saying it could work."

"How would we get our hands on it?" I ask her. "Vance never comes to the boutique. Oddly enough, Ivy doesn't seem to either. The only way we'd see Vance again was if we went to his house. He's not going to let us in after today."

"Then we need to find another way." Riley grabs another slice of pizza and bites into it.

"What about Detective Bilson?" I ask.

"Garrett would never help us. The guy is too straightlaced. Can you imagine him sneaking into someone's home?" She scoffs.

"I don't mean ask him to help us steal it." I roll my eyes at her. Sometimes her need to pretend she doesn't like Garrett makes her act completely irrationally. "If we tell him about the will and how Ivy tried to steal it, he might look into it."

"Might being the key word there." She points her pizza at me. "He's content to think he's closed this case, Hailey. He's not going to pursue a new lead just because we tell him to."

If *we* tell him to, no. But if Riley tells him to… We might have a chance. "What if Rumor Robin writes a column about the missing will?" Ben doesn't know Riley is Rumor Robin, so I can't come out and tell her to do it.

"No one knows who Rumor Robin is, though," Ben says. "How would we tell her?"

I need a plausible excuse for how we could pass information to an unknown person. "What if we start a rumor. We get people talking. It will most likely get back to Rumor Robin, and she can expose this whole scandal with Simone's will."

"If it even is something scandalous," Ben says.

"It's worth a shot. Don't you think?" I look to Riley.

"I like it," she says, which means she'll write the column.

By midday Thursday, the new Rumor Robin column comes out, and the entire town is in an uproar talking about the secret will and what it could possibly mean for Simone's murder. Laurent has been in his office all day, and Ivy has even dropped by to see him. She stormed right past me to his office. I guess she hasn't forgiven me for my part in exposing her theft to Vance Brooks. I don't feel the least bit guilty, though, since she's the one who took it upon herself to steal from her brother-in-law's home.

Laurent offers Leslie and me overtime if we agree to eat our lunches at the boutique and not take our breaks. I'm happy to accept the offer since I need the money. So Riley and Ben both drop by at lunchtime to see me.

"I can't believe Rumor Robin really heard about the rumor and wrote a column on it," Ben says.

"I can." I give Riley the briefest of smiles. "I talked to Pete Modell this morning. I figured he'd spread the rumor quicker than anyone since he knows everyone in town."

"That was smart thinking," Riley says.

"I'm almost certain Pete knows who Rumor Robin is," Ben says. "Like most people, I thought it was him for a while, but once he left town to do community service, I figured we were all wrong about that."

"Well, if Pete does know who Rumor Robin is, I don't think he'll tell," Riley says.

"Probably not. I can see him being in on the secret, though," I say.

Detective Bilson walks into the boutique, and when he sees the three of us together, he shakes his head. "Are you three behind this?" He places a copy of the *Rockland Record* on the counter.

"You do know you can read that on your phone, right?" I ask him.

"Just answer the question, Hailey."

"I'm pretty sure Samuel Montage is behind the *Rockland Record*." I turn to Riley. "Did I get your uncle's name right?"

"Yup." She cocks her head at Detective Bilson. "It must really irk you that a gossip columnist knows more about your investigation than you do."

"The missing will has nothing to do with the murder."

"Really?" I ask. "Isn't money the biggest motive for murder? How can you not think it has anything to do with Simone's death?"

"Maxwell Decker stands nothing to gain in that will."

I cross my arms and smirk. "Hmm, it seems like I've been trying to tell you all along that he has no motive. I guess I should be happy you're finally starting to see that."

"I'm not saying he didn't have a motive. I'm saying the motive wasn't money."

"Okay, what was it then?" I ask, lowering my arms at my sides.

"I'm not discussing it with you."

"Why are you here if not to discuss the case with me?"

"I told you already. I want to know if you were behind the gossip column."

"No. I was not." I'm careful to phrase it in a way that's honest. I didn't write the column. Riley did. Sure, I gave her the idea, but she's the one who actually followed through with it.

"And you know nothing about it?"

"I read the column today like everyone else," I say, once again sticking to the truth. Or at least the part of the truth I want him to know.

His jaw clenches.

"Oh, but you might be interested to know that Laurent and his wife are both in his office right now. You know, in case you have any questions you'd like them to answer about this will." I can't believe I have to tell this man how to do his job.

He glares at me for a moment and then looks at Riley. "What are you smiling at?"

"I was just remembering the time you gave that speech at school and your fly was down. Remember? You thought everyone loved what you had to say because we all clapped and cheered, but then you realized we were laughing at you." She starts laughing. "Good times."

Detective Bilson's face turns bright red, and he opens his mouth to say something but stops.

"You're wondering if I thought of that because your fly is down right now, aren't you? You're dying to check." Riley raises one eyebrow in challenge.

"Excuse me," Detective Bilson says, pushing past us toward Laurent's office.

"It's not down," Riley calls after him.

I smack her arm. "You are awful to him."

"He deserves it."

More like she was scared that he was asking questions about Rumor Robin. If anyone in town is going to figure out it's Riley, it will be Garrett Bilson. He's known her the longest.

Detective Bilson comes rushing back out into the boutique. "I thought you said Laurent and his wife were in his office."

"They are," I say.

"No, they're not."

If they're not there, they snuck out the back through the storage room that's off-limits. Why would they do that?

CHAPTER SIX

Leslie marches over to us. "What do you mean Laurent isn't back there? He has to be. If he left, he'd have to come through the boutique, and I'm positive he didn't."

"That means they left through the crime scene," I say. "Makes you wonder why?" And if they left in a hurry because they heard Detective Bilson's voice. "Think they're trying to avoid you?" I ask him.

He lets out a long sigh. "Call me the second either one of them returns."

I nod. I might give him a hard time, but I'm not going to impede his investigation in any way.

He hurries out of the boutique.

Leslie walks over to me. "You don't think Laurent did anything wrong, do you?"

"I don't know. The Rumor Robin column made it seem like he might have had a reason to want his sister out of the way."

"I can't see Laurent hurting anyone. It's just not his personality." She looks down at the floor. "What about Jesse? He's called out of work every day since the murder."

Jesse is still a teenager in high school. I'm willing to bet his parents won't let him step foot in this place after Simone was murdered here. "He's just a kid. I'm sure he's scared."

"Not Jesse. He loves fashion. It's all he's ever wanted to do. He's going to attend fashion school after he graduates. And he adores Ruby Redford. He'd never miss an opportunity to run into her here." Leslie shakes her head. "Something is wrong there."

I look to Ben and Riley. "Leslie, I'll go talk to Jesse after work today and see what's going on."

"You will?"

"Yeah. I'll make sure he's okay and that he didn't have anything to do with Simone's murder."

"How do you do this, Hailey? I'm so freaked out about everything. You and I were here when Simone died. We were in the building with the killer. How doesn't that totally terrify you?"

Because it's not the first time this has happened to me. I've come to learn that at any given moment, you could be in the presence of someone who has taken or plans to take a life. I place a hand on Leslie's shoulder. "Try not to think about it. You and I were together in the boutique. Safety in numbers, right?"

"Great. You leave me every day when you take your lunch break. And I'm here with Laurent, who, according to you, might be the killer."

Okay, so maybe my words weren't the comfort I'd hoped they'd be. "I'm doing everything I can to figure out what really happened on Monday."

"I knew you didn't think the delivery guy was the killer," she says. "I could tell."

I need to work on my acting skills. "I'm not saying he didn't do it. I'm saying I can't find a motive for him to want Simone dead."

"He either had one we can't see or someone hired him to kill Simone," Riley says, using the story we've been telling people. "We'll find out, though."

Leslie gestures between us. "So you three solve crimes in your spare time?"

"Sort of," I say. "Did Jesse already call out today?"

She nods. "He texted me earlier."

"Is he giving a reason?"

"He said he doesn't feel well, but I know that's just a lie."

Most likely. "We'll get to the bottom of it. For now, let's focus on getting through our shift here."

"It doesn't help that it's so quiet in here today. What happened to all the customers?"

That's a good question. I thought the rumor about the will would have brought more people into the boutique looking to see Laurent and get some insight as to whether Rumor Robin is right about Simone's secret will. But the crowd is staying outside on the street.

"Can you guys go find out what everyone is talking about out there?" I ask Ben and Riley.

"On it," Riley says. "Let's go, Ben." She drags him toward the door. He looks over her head at me, and I mouth, "Sorry." Riley is a force to be reckoned with.

Leslie and I wait inside, watching through the front window. Riley and Ben make their way through the crowd, talking to just about everyone. By the time they come back inside, they look frazzled.

"People are crazy in mobs like that," Riley says.

"What did they say?" I ask.

"There are rumors about Simone hiding her money from both Laurent and Vance. People think that's why she needed the secret will. They believe she had a secret bank account where she stashed a ton of money to keep all to herself."

"But she'd have to pay taxes on it, so how would she keep that from her husband?" I ask.

"That was my question as well," Ben says. "The theory is that she had the account in another name."

"What name?" If I hadn't met Ruby Redford myself, I'd think she was actually Simone's alias. Simone was big on fashion. It could have made sense that the designs they were selling under the name Ruby Redford were hers all along, and Simone didn't want Laurent to find out. But I met Ruby in the flesh. She was even here when Simone was murdered.

"No one has any idea what name she might have used."

We don't have the resources to find out either. "Riley, I hate to say it, but I think we need to take this to Detective Bilson. He's the only one who can find out if Simone has a secret bank account under a different name."

"You're kidding, right? Garrett is never going to follow a lead he got from a mob of people speculating about the will. He's not the type to listen to others to begin with, but considering these are civilians with no actual knowledge of the murder or Simone Vincent, Garrett will never entertain their theories."

"We need to make him. By any means necessary."

She widens her eyes at me, picking up on the fact that I'm implying we might need to out her as Rumor Robin. "No. Absolutely not. I won't do it, Hailey."

Ben narrows his eyes at us. "What am I missing here?"

"I have to get back to work. My uncle might be my boss, but I still have a job to do." She leaves in a hurry, and for the first time since I've met her, I'm pretty sure she's mad at me.

Ben pulls me away from Leslie. "Care to fill me in on what just happened? I'm more than a little confused by all that."

"I can't." This isn't my secret to share. Riley trusted me with this information right off the bat, and I've never understood why, but I refuse to betray her trust to anyone. Not even to Ben. "I'm sorry, but I just can't."

"Okay. I get it. It's between you and Riley."

"Thank you for understanding."

He squeezes my elbow. "I should go."

"You're not mad at me, too, are you?"

"No. We're good." He leaves, giving me a small smile as he lets the door close behind him.

"I can't wait for this day to be over. I just want to go home and crawl into bed," Leslie says.

"You and me both."

At quitting time, I get into my car, ready to go see Jesse to find out why he keeps calling out of work, but I don't know his address or even his last name. I lean my head on the steering wheel. A few seconds later, someone taps on my window, making me jump in my seat.

Pete Modell holds up a hand in apology as I lower the window. "I didn't mean to scare you, Hailey. I just wanted to make sure you were okay."

"It's all right. I got into an argument with Riley today, and I need her help with something. I'm just upset because I don't know what to do."

"Is it anything I can help you with?"

I look up into his big, caring eyes. "You don't happen to know Jesse, the kid who works in the boutique with me, do you?"

"Yes. Jesse Merrill."

I start to perk up already. "Do you know where he lives?"

"He lives at home with his parents on Bishop Avenue. They're the navy blue house with the white shutters. You can't miss it."

I smile at him. "Pete, you really are a lifesaver. I owe you one. Or three or five. I've lost count at this point."

"I'm happy to help, Hailey." He gives me a wave as I pull out of the parking lot.

I haven't lived in town for long, but I'm starting to learn my way around. I know where Bishop Avenue is, so I don't even have to put it into my navigation on my phone. Like Pete said, there's only one navy blue house with white shutters. I park on the street in front of it and walk up to the front door. There's no doorbell, so I knock.

Jesse answers, giving me a curious look. "Hailey, right?"

"That's right. I wanted to check on you. Leslie's been worried since you've called out a few times."

"Did Laurent send you to make sure I'm actually sick and not just bailing on work?"

"No. I swear. It was Leslie and me worrying about you." I look over my shoulder to make sure no one is walking along the street. "Jesse, this isn't the first time I've been around when a murder happened. I know how scary it is. And if that's why you're staying away from the boutique, I completely understand."

"It's my mom. She doesn't want me going back there. I've tried to tell her it's perfectly safe since the police caught the guy who killed Simone, but she's not so sure they have the right person."

"Why would she think Maxwell Decker isn't the murderer?" To an outsider, it should look like an open and shut case since Maxwell was discovered with the body and holding the murder weapon.

"My mom likes to watch true crime shows. She said the delivery guy had no motive to kill a woman he didn't know."

Oh boy. Maybe it's not a good thing that true crime shows are so addicting.

"She said in cases where wealthy people are murdered, it's usually a family member who killed them because they stand the most to gain from the death. She said the latest Rumor Robin column proves that's what happened to Simone."

Great. So it was my idea for Riley to write the column that's making Jesse's mother suspicious. All I'd intended to do was tip off Detective Bilson, but I should have known the column would make everyone in town suspect a family member of killing Simone. "Is your mom worried Laurent might be the killer?"

Jesse looks down at his dress socks. That's when I realize that this kid is dressed as if he's going out on the town even though he's lounging around at home. He really does love fashion. "Laurent's been really good to me. I can't bring myself to believe he had anything to do with Simone's death, but I can't convince my mom of that."

"It's okay, Jesse. I'm not sure any of us know what to make of this."

"So many people disliked Simone. She was nasty to me, too. And all I ever did was what she asked of me. I never questioned her or anything. But she'd find fault in the way I handled the designers or the fact that I'd work on my designs during my breaks."

"I didn't know Simone gave you a hard time."

He bobs one shoulder. "I think she wanted to be a designer but couldn't cut it. That's why she and Laurent opened the boutique. But it makes her really critical of other designers. She's lucky she landed Ruby Redford. She's going to be a big name one day. I can tell. And now that Simone isn't holding her back anymore, I bet it happens soon."

"How was Simone holding Ruby back?"

"Well, Simone always stocked everything Ruby gave her."

"Isn't that a good thing?"

"Yeah, definitely. But Ruby deserves a much bigger setting for her designs. She should be in Paris or Milan, but she's stuck in Rockland for some reason, selling her work for peanuts in a tiny boutique. She deserves better."

"Did she and Simone get along?"

"As well as anyone could get along with Simone."

"Jesse, who are you talking to?" A woman comes up behind him and glares at me.

"Hi, I'm Hailey. I work with Jesse at the boutique."

"He doesn't work there anymore."

"Yes, I do, Mom." He rolls his eyes but keeps his head facing me so his mother doesn't see.

"That's what you think. I'm not letting you go back to that place after that horrible woman was killed there."

"I'm sure it's scary for you to think about Jesse being somewhere a murder occurred," I say.

"See." She holds a hand out in my direction. "She gets it. Why don't you?" she asks Jesse.

"It's my job, Mom. I have to work there. I need the job experience for my resume and my application to fashion school."

"You need a real job. Not one in fashion. There's no money there."

"Simone Vincent was crazy rich," Jesse says.

"Not from her designs or that boutique!" Jesse's mother holds her arms out at her sides. "Look around. You're not getting a huge inheritance like Simone got. You need to face reality."

"Reality is I don't want to stay in this tiny little nothing of a town. I want to live in Paris and design dresses for celebrities."

"You've got your head in the clouds, Jesse. I'm telling you that woman's death was the best thing that could have happened to you. Without this job, you're going to have to listen to reason. Go to college and get a degree in a real field."

Jesse pushes past her and storms up the stairs.

Mrs. Merrill shakes her head. "He'll thank me one day when he can actually afford to pay his bills." She closes the door in my face, leaving me to wonder what she expects him to thank her for. Ruining his dreams? And how exactly is she responsible when she said it was Simone's death that was the best thing that could have happened to Jesse. The only way that could be the case is if she killed Simone.

CHAPTER SEVEN

I'm dying to talk to Riley, but I still haven't heard from her since I suggested she come clean to Detective Bilson about being the author of the Rumor Robin column. I use the little money I have and buy Chinese food to bring to her townhouse.

When she opens the door, I hold up the bag. "Peace offering."

"Are there egg rolls?"

"Yes."

"Fortune cookies?"

"I asked for extra."

She steps aside to let me in. Marley hurries over to say hello to me.

"Hey, buddy. At least someone is happy to see me."

"If you wanted someone to fawn all over you, you should have gone to Ben's. I'm mad at you about that, too."

I put the Chinese food on the kitchen table. "About what exactly?"

"You kissed him. Or he kissed you. He told me. Why am I hearing this from him and not you?"

"Sorry. I still don't know what to make of whatever it is that's going on between us. I'm sort of afraid talking about it out loud will jinx it." I sit down and start pulling the food out of the bag.

Riley grabs bottles of water from the refrigerator and sits with me. "The guy is totally into you. Aside from killing someone in front of him, I'm not sure you could do anything to screw it up."

"Why are you really mad at me?" I ask.

"You know why. You suggested I tell Garret I'm Rumor Robin."

"Don't you think on some level he already knows?"

"Why do you think I'm working so hard to prove to him that I'm not. Of course, he suspects. He knows me too well."

"Because he's been in love with you since you were in kindergarten," I say under my breath.

"I heard that. And you're wrong."

"How do you explain him wearing the handkerchief you made him in kindergarten in his senior yearbook photo?" She only recently discovered this when she showed me her high school yearbook from Garrett's senior year.

She bobs a shoulder. "That was a long time ago, and it probably didn't mean anything at the time either. Maybe he didn't have another handkerchief for his jacket pocket."

I level my gaze on her. "If I can somehow prove he still has it, would you admit he likes you?"

"Sure because he definitely doesn't still have it, and you'd never prove it anyway." She opens the container of lo mein and digs right in.

I bite my egg roll. "Challenge accepted," I say with my mouth full.

"I'm glad Ben isn't here to witness you talking around your food like that."

"According to you, he wouldn't care."

She rolls her eyes.

Now that things seem to be back to normal between us, I fill her in on my conversation with Jesse and his mother.

"You don't think she killed Simone to get Jesse to give up his dream of going into the fashion industry, do you? I mean that's crazy."

"Isn't murder crazy to begin with?" I ask.

"Okay, yes. And I suppose if she did kill Simone, she wouldn't want her son going to the Boutique because she wouldn't want any connection to the murder at all."

"Or she's afraid Jesse would pick up on some clue she was there."

"A clue like what? Even if she wears strong perfume, the scent would be long gone by now."

I shrug. "I don't know what kind of clue. I'm thinking out loud."

"Does any part of you think Jesse could be the killer?" she asks. "He could be hiding behind his mother right now to avoid suspicion. Or she could know he's the killer and is covering for him."

"Neither had any idea I was stopping by to talk to Jesse, so I don't think they could have pulled off a ruse like that on the spot." I finish my egg roll. "Besides, Jesse was with Ruby Redford in Simone's office when Simone was killed. He has an alibi."

"Which begs the question, why were they waiting in her office if she wasn't even there?"

"Maybe she went to sign for the delivery and told them to go wait in her office. I'll have to ask one of them to find out for sure."

"You do realize if that's the case, Maxwell Decker looks even guiltier. If that's possible."

I get what she's saying. It means he would have already been there at the time of Simone's murder. He told the police he found her when he arrived. "Should we have Pete in on these meetings?" I ask. He's Maxwell's friend, and I'm sure he'd want to know what's going on with the investigation.

"Normally, I'd say yes. I like Pete. But he's too close to this. Max is his friend, and I'm not sure Pete would be able to think rationally because he'd be too busy trying to clear Max's name."

Marley walks into the kitchen when she hears Riley tear open the fortune cookie. He meows, and she breaks off a tiny piece of the cookie for him. He takes it, chews loudly, and then walks back out of the kitchen.

"Cats are such users. I swear he only ever bothers with humans when he wants something."

Marley is actually pretty cuddly for a cat. But I suppose that benefits him as well, so I can see what Riley's saying about him.

There's a knock on Riley's door, and she looks at me. "Did you invite Ben?"

"No," I say.

She gets up to answer the door. "Oh goodie."

I don't have to ask who she saw through the peephole. I stand up to greet Detective Bilson with her.

"Garrett," she says.

"Riles."

He only calls her that when he's not officially on the clock.

"There's still some Chinese food if you're hungry." I hitch a thumb toward the kitchen.

"No, thank you. I already ate." He looks really uncomfortable. He turns to face Riley. "I need to talk to you. Alone."

"I'll be in the kitchen," I say, already backing into it.

They walk into the living room, Riley giving me a questioning look on the way. I shrug in response because I have no idea why Detective Bilson is here.

"What's up?" Riley begins. "What is that?"

I hate not being able to see what's happening. I try to peer around the corner. Detective Bilson has his back to me in his seat on the couch, but I can tell he's handing something to Marley. "I'm still trying to make up for not sharing my food with Marley that night I had to sleep on your couch."

"So you brought him cat treats?" Riley asks.

No. He doesn't like her at all. I shake my head. My goodness, how is she so blind?

Detective Bilson clears his throat. "I need to ask you something."

Is he going to ask her out?

"And I need you to give me a straight answer."

"I already dislike this, but go on." Riley sees me, and her eyes widen slightly, making Detective Bilson turn his head in my direction. I duck back into the kitchen. "I thought I saw a spider," Riley says.

"Oh." Detective Bilson is quiet for a moment.

"Spit it out already, Garrett."

"Who writes the Rumor Robin columns? Your uncle owns the paper, and he's not talking. But I'm certain you know."

"It's me," I say, coming out of the kitchen.

Detective Bilson shakes his head. "Come on, Hailey. You just moved here. You can't be Rumor Robin."

"Rumor Robin isn't one person. Several people write the columns. We get inside information from sources who write in with anonymous tips. Then someone on the team of writers puts the column together. That's how it works. I wrote the last column because I found out about the secret will, and I wanted to get the information to you. I figured you'd be upset if I went to you directly with what I knew, so I opted to do it through the column instead." I hold my arms out at my sides for a moment and let them fall. "Now you know."

Detective Bilson turns to Riley. "Do you have anything to say?"

"Nope." She holds up a finger. "Actually, yes. You can't tell anyone. This secret will ruin the paper, and that's my uncle you'd be messing with. I'd never forgive you."

Detective Bilson lowers his head. "I can't believe you'd think I would ask you to share a secret with me and then I'd turn around and tell people. Why do you think so little of me, Riley?"

This is heartbreaking to watch. Inside my head, I'm screaming for her to tell him the truth. He'd keep her secret. I'm sure of it. But she's not budging.

"I guess this is the perfect opportunity for you to prove you're trustworthy."

"I'm not sure what I ever did to make you think otherwise." He stands up and starts for the door. "Hailey, the will was smart thinking. I'll look into it and see who might have paid Maxwell Decker to murder Simone."

He still thinks Maxwell was the actual killer.

"In the future, come directly to me with your theories, though. Don't stir up the entire town to get a message to me."

"Sorry," I say.

He walks out without another word to Riley. I close the door behind him.

"Now you're really forgiven," Riley says. "Thanks for covering for me."

"Why didn't you tell him? He came here thinking it was you. He had already accepted it, but you let me take the fall."

"You're the one who stepped in and claimed responsibility. I didn't ask you to do that."

"I know, but I thought when you saw he wasn't upset, you'd come clean. You hurt him with all that trustworthy stuff you said."

"You're acting like Garrett is your best friend, not me. Why are you taking his side?"

"I'm not. I think your life would be easier and possibly better if you were honest with him about a lot of things."

"That's not for you to decide."

I nod. "But you forget that when I first got to Rockland, you conveniently ditched me so Ben would take me out. You meddled back then, and I knew you thought you were helping, so I didn't hold it against you. This is no different."

She lets out a deep breath. "I get what you're saying, but this is so much more complicated, Hailey. I don't know how to make you understand that."

"I guess I don't understand how you can ignore the possibility of a future with someone who has seen you through your worst times and still looks at you like you're the most incredible human being alive."

"He doesn't…" She shakes her head. "Do you know why I started the Rumor Robin column?"

"No." We're still standing at her front door, so I shift my weight from one foot to the other.

"Because growing up in a town where everyone knows you and everything you do means you have no privacy. No secrets. Being Rumor Robin, I have something no one knows about. I finally have a secret. I like that. It's why I chose to share it with you. You didn't grow up here. You don't know all my other secrets. You only know what I chose to share with you."

I bob my head. "That makes sense. And I'll continue to pretend I'm one of the Rumor Robin writers for as long as you want me to."

"Thank you." She reaches out and hugs me.

"I should head home."

"You're welcome to stay."

"I appreciate it, but I haven't checked in with Ben at all, and I want to call it an early night."

"Okay. Any idea what lead you want to pursue tomorrow?"

"Yeah, I think I need to talk to Ruby Redford and find out if she and Jesse saw Simone moments before the murder."

"Ask her to come to the boutique, and I'll meet you there to talk to her."

"Sounds good."

I leave, and I'm almost home when I notice the patrol car behind me. I park in front of my apartment and go inside, leaving the door open for Detective Bilson, who is following me. "I'd offer you a drink, but my refrigerator is empty. All I have is tap water." I gesture to the kitchen sink.

Detective Bilson is still standing in the doorway. "May I come in?"

"Sure."

He steps inside and closes the door behind him.

I sit down on the arm of the couch. "What's this about?"

"I know you lied. I know you're not Rumor Robin."

I start to protest, but he puts up a hand to stop me.

"I'm not an idiot, Hailey. I've had my suspicions for a while now, but she's cleverly written things to throw me off her path."

"I don't know what you mean." I'm not sure why I'm still denying it since he clearly knows the truth, but I did promise Riley I'd continue to claim I was the author of the gossip column.

"I'm talking about Riley being Rumor Robin. I know her. I've always known her. She used to write stories for the school newspaper. Her writing style hasn't changed all that much."

"I will not confirm or deny if Riley is one of the Rumor Robin writers."

He smiles and shakes his head. "You're a good friend. I'm glad because Riles deserves that kind of loyalty."

"Is this really why you followed me home?" I ask.

"No. I wanted to tell you to stop investigating. Like I said at Riley's place, one of the family members might be behind all this, but Maxwell Decker is the one who committed the murder."

"No, he didn't."

Detective Bilson drags a hand through his hair. "He's Pete Modell's friend, and Pete has come to your rescue a few times. I understand that you want to help him clear his friend's name, but it's not going to happen. I'm sorry."

"You really think you're going to get one of the family members in the will to admit to hiring Maxwell to kill Simone?" I ask.

"I don't think that part will be easy by any means, but if that's what actually happened, I'm going to do my best to prove it." His phone rings, and he pulls it from his pocket. "Detective Bilson," he answers. His gaze goes to me. "When? Does she have any idea where he might have gone? Okay, I'm on it." He hangs up. "Looks like Jesse Merrill ran away this evening. His mother said he packed a bag and drove away."

Jesse is eighteen, a legal adult. There's not much his mother could have done to stop him. "She's asking the police to find him?"

He nods. "She said she's afraid for his safety. She thinks he knows more about the murder than he's letting on."

"Is she worried he can identify the killer or that he is the killer?" I ask.

"She's not sure."

CHAPTER EIGHT

Since Jesse isn't a missing person, given he drove off and told his mother he was leaving, there isn't too much Detective Bilson can do. But Mrs. Merrill gave the police reason to suspect Jesse could have been involved or knows about the murder, which makes him someone they want to find. Detective Bilson said they'd put out a BOLO on Jesse's car so they can bring him in to the station if he's spotted.

When I tell Leslie about it at work on Friday, she's shocked. "Jesse wouldn't kill Simone. Besides, he was with Ruby when it happened. They're each other's alibis. His mother is just saying this to get the police to bring him home since she can't report him missing." Leslie wipes a tear from her eye. "What kind of parent does that to their child? All because she doesn't approve of his career choice. It's absurd. Completely absurd. I mean to prefer to see your only child in an orange prison jumpsuit as opposed to working in fashion…" She scoffs. "What is wrong with people?"

There's a loaded question. I feel bad for Jesse, but solving this murder seems like the more pressing issue. I offer Leslie a bob of my head to acknowledge her comments, and then I walk to the bathroom to call Ruby Redford, whose number I looked up last night.

"Hello?" she answers.

"Hi, Ms. Redford, this is Hailey Hart from Belle Boutique."

"Yes."

"I was wondering if you'd be able to stop in to the shop today. There's something I'd like to discuss with you."

"I didn't have an appointment with anyone from the boutique today."

"I know. Now that Simone is gone, we have to get a few things in order. I know it's all very last minute, but I'm sure you can understand that extenuating circumstances do create these necessary last-minute changes." I hope I'm making even a shred of sense. I'm not sure what I'm saying at this point. I was hoping to talk circles around her to get her to agree to come in, but I think it's worked on me instead.

"What time do you need me to come in?"

"Any time that's convenient for you is fine. We're happy to work around your schedule since this is last minute."

She huffs into the phone. "It looks like I can make it at ten o'clock."

"Great. We'll see you then." I end the call before she can change her mind or ask any other questions.

When I step out of the bathroom, Laurent and his wife are in his office. I never followed up with Detective Bilson to find out how they left without Leslie and me seeing them. I move toward the office to eavesdrop.

"She was selling her own designs. This is unbelievable," Laurent says.

"I still don't understand why she'd hide behind Ruby," Ivy says.

"I don't know, but we need to talk to Ruby and find out."

If he calls Ruby after I just spoke with her, Ruby will know I lied to her.

"This is why Ruby had two lines, Ruby and Red. One belonged to Simone, and the other was Ruby's own line," Laurent said. "Simone must have been trying to pull one over on me. By not selling under her own name, the money she made wasn't connected to the boutique or the business at all. She pocketed it all without Vance or anyone knowing."

"Ruby knew," Ivy says.

"Yes, I suppose they were thick as thieves."

"But then why didn't Simone leave Ruby anything in her will. Why did she pour all the money into releasing the line under her real name?"

That's where Simone left her money? She put it into an account to release her own designs into the world? No wonder she kept this a secret. She left her family with nothing. All she cared about was making a name for herself so she'd live on after her death. This has to be motive. Except Laurent and Ivy knew nothing about it until now. Neither one of them could have killed Simone over this.

I'm starting to think that the reason they ran when they heard Detective Bilson yesterday was because Ivy didn't give Vance Brooks the real flash drive. I think she gave him a different one and kept the will for herself. She and Laurent probably had it on them here yesterday and assumed Detective Bilson was here because Vance Brooks reported what they'd done to the authorities.

Does Vance even know it's the wrong flash drive in his possession? Has he even tried to view what's on it yet?

The door to Laurent's office opens, and I come face-to-face with my boss. I jump. "Oh, you scared me. I was about to knock," I lie.

"Did you need something?"

"Yes, um, I wanted to tell you that Jesse Merrill is missing." I hope he'll care enough about that to put off calling Ruby Redford until I can come up with a plan.

"Missing?"

"Yes, his mother called the police last night. I figured you'd want to know since he works here. I guess he packed his things and took off late last night."

"Why would he do that unless…?" Ivy gawks at her husband. "Wasn't Jesse with Ruby when Simone was killed?"

She must think Jesse was in on this with Ruby. She might even suspect Jesse and Ruby killed Simone together and then used each other as alibis. That would actually be really smart.

"Do the police have any idea where he is?" Laurent asks me.

"I don't know, but they want to ask you some questions. Detective Bilson was here asking to have you come to the station immediately." Hopefully, that will keep Laurent and Ivy busy while I talk to Ruby. Unless they call her on the way. I can't let that happen.

"He was just here?"

"Yes, looking for you both, actually. I said I'd come find you, but he ran out in a hurry, mumbling something about Ruby Redford."

Laurent and Ivy exchange a look.

"I'm not sure what Detective Bilson thinks is the connection between those two, though. It's not like there's any evidence to suggest Ruby and Jesse could have harmed Simone. I mean what reason would they have, right? They both worked with her, and Simone took care of Ruby." I look at the time on my phone screen. "Anyway, I told him I'd make sure you went right down to the station. He seemed like he was in a big hurry, and you know how cranky he gets when he's upset, so I'd go straight there if I were you." I finally stop talking and stare at them.

"I'll pay you and Leslie to work through lunch again today. I don't know what time I'll be back."

"Sure. Whatever you need," I call after them as they hurry out. I smile to myself, relieved my plan worked. I doubt they'll share the contents of that flash drive with anyone since the will essentially gives Simone's money to herself. I wonder who she listed as the recipient of the money the clothing line makes. That's probably the real killer. If they were, in fact, aware of this plan all along, which I'm assuming they were since Simone had to have it all set up already.

I doubt Laurent would leave the flash drive behind or his office unlocked again, but I try the knob anyway. Locked. I head back into the boutique.

"Hey, do you know what's up with Laurent?" Leslie asks. "He and his wife ran out of here."

"They were called down to the police station."

"Did they do something? Is it about them leaving through the storage room yesterday?" Poor Leslie. She's freaked out by all of this still.

"I don't know. I just conveyed a message. Listen, since it's not busy, why don't you take a break. Go get brunch. The diner is probably not crowded right now, and we're going to have to work through lunch again."

"Are you sure?"

"Yeah. You've been so great showing me around. I'd like to be able to do something for you in return, so go. Have some pancakes for me." I smile at her.

"Well, okay. If you're sure, I won't turn down pancakes and coffee. Do you want me to bring back anything for you?"

I can't afford anything. "No, I'm good. I had a big breakfast this morning." Yup, a whole slice of toast.

"Okay, I'll be quick."

"No rush. There's no one here anyway," I tell her.

I watch her leave. I have about half an hour until Ruby is supposed to be here. I have to hope Detective Bilson can stall Laurent and Ivy Vincent long enough for me to talk to Ruby. I have a bad feeling this could all blow up in my face though, so I call Detective Bilson.

"Hailey?" he answers.

"You put my number in your phone?" I ask.

"You should be surprised you're not on my speed dial at this point with the way you're always poking your nose into my investigations."

"Speaking of that. I just overheard Laurent and Ivy Vincent. They have the will. I think Ivy gave Vance Brooks a different flash drive."

"Why would they do that?"

"Because Simone left all her money to her own clothing line. She basically screwed over Laurent and her husband. I think Laurent and Ivy ran yesterday because they thought you'd found out what they'd done. Laurent might have the flash drive on him now, or it's locked in his office. You've got to nail them on this."

"Do you think they had anything to do with Simone's murder?"

"No. They had no idea what was in the will, and if they did, they never would have killed her. They don't want this will to come to light."

"Okay, I'll call them both in."

"You don't have to. I just sent them both to you."

"You're kidding me. How did you manage to pull that off?"

"I'm not even sure, but they're on their way now. They're convinced Ruby Redford was helping Simone secretly sell her own work so Simone could pocket the money without Laurent or Vance finding out."

"How would they come to that conclusion? Did Ruby say something?"

"No. I think the will contains a confession about the Ruby Redford clothing lines. You need to get ahold of that flash drive."

"I'm on it." At first, I think he's ended the call because it goes silent, but then he says, "Hailey, thank you." Then he really does hang up.

I breathe a little easier knowing Detective Bilson will detain the Vincents for me while I question Ruby.

Ruby arrives a few minutes early. She looks around the shop, possibly taking inventory of her designs. "It's so quiet in here."

"Yes, it's a slow day."

"I'd think Fridays would be busier than Mondays."

"You never can tell, can you?"

"Where's Laurent?"

"Oh, the meeting is actually with me. Laurent had to step out."

She looks me up and down. "What about Jesse?"

She knows Jesse by name. Maybe Laurent and Ivy were right to suspect those two were working together.

"He's in school until three," I say, trying to find out if she knows Jesse ran away.

"Shame. He always makes me coffee." She removes the driving gloves from her hands. "Tell me why I'm here."

"It's about your two design lines, Ruby and Red."

"What about them?"

"Apparently, Simone left some paperwork that describes the relationship you two had. She is claiming ownership of one of the two lines, saying she used your name to release her own line."

"Her designs? Well, sometimes we'd brainstorm together. Simone liked to be part of the creative process, but the end products were all mine. Where did you say you heard this?"

"From Simone herself. She left paperwork documenting her claims."

"That's absurd. Simone was very good to me. She always showcased my designs and made me her top designer. I assure you they were my designs, though. You must be misinterpreting this document you claim to have read. I'd like to see it."

"I'm afraid I don't have it. Laurent does. But you said she was very good to you."

"Yes. Very. We had a great relationship."

"What was the nature of your meeting on Monday?" I ask.

"Brainstorming, sharing ideas, it's what Simone and I did. It was quite enjoyable. Sometimes Jesse would sit in on our meetings."

"I suppose that's why he escorted you to Simone's office," I say. She nods. "Yes."

"Can you tell me what happened Monday when you went to Simone's office?"

"I'll try. I admit it's difficult to think about."

"I'm sure."

"Jesse and I were discussing a design he's working on. I was giving him tips, and I heard the back door chime."

"What chime?" I ask.

She puts a hand on her chest. "I forgot you haven't been here long. The back door has a chime on it. The delivery guys have the keycode to get inside, but the door chimes to let the employees know they're getting a delivery," Ruby says. "I heard the chime, and I guess Simone did too because she went to get the delivery."

"Where were you when you heard the door chime?"

"At Simone's open office door. Jesse suggested we go inside to wait for Simone since it would only take a moment for her to sign for the package."

This isn't good at all. It's going to make it look like Maxwell lied about finding Simone dead. I highly doubt Detective Bilson will stop to consider someone else used the keycode to open the back door and pretend to be a delivery man. It also makes me question if Maxwell was setup from the start.

CHAPTER NINE

Ruby Redford cocks her head at me. "I thought we were going to discuss my contract with Bell Boutique."

"Yes, um, Laurent just wanted me to make sure you were still willing to sell your designs here now that Simone is gone."

Ruby reaches inside her purse, pulls out a tissue, and dabs the corners of her eyes with it. "I admit it will be very different without Simone, but I think she'd want me to stay on here."

I nod.

"And I like working with Jesse. He's so eager to learn all he can. I see a lot of myself in him. I'd like to be here as sort of a mentor to him."

"Oh, well, Jesse actually hasn't been here since Monday."

"Did he quit?" She furrows her brow.

"Not officially, but his mother reported that he ran away from home."

"Why?"

"I believe it was because his parents didn't support his dream of becoming a fashion designer."

Ruby tosses the tissue into her purse. "That's ridiculous. That boy has real promise. To discourage that kind of talent is a disgrace."

"Well, hopefully, he'll come back and prove his parents wrong," I say.

"I certainly hope so. If he does return, please tell him to call me." She reaches into her purse again and pulls out a business card. She scribbles something on the back of it and hands it to me. "Give this to him for me, please. Everyone needs to know they have someone who believes in them, and if he needs that person to be me, then so be it."

"That's very kind of you, Ms. Redford."

"It's what Simone did for me," she says.

I bob my head and watch her walk out.

Well, that didn't exactly go the way I envisioned. I was hoping she'd be able to give me some clue as to what happened Monday evening, but she only heard the chime of the back door. I can't exactly go to Detective Bilson with this information.

Leslie returns from her brunch break, smiling from ear to ear. "I had the best omelet ever."

"I thought you said you wanted pancakes."

"I thought so too, but that man of yours was there, and he was eating this delicious looking omelet. I asked him what it was and ordered the same for myself."

"Ben was at the diner?" I ask.

"Yup."

"Alone?"

"No, there was a woman with him."

"Seriously?" I shriek.

She laughs and holds up both hands. "No, sorry. I was joking. But wow. I guess you really like him if you're that upset by the thought of him eating breakfast with another woman."

"Sorry."

"No, I'm sorry. I didn't realize it would upset you like that."

I still don't know why he'd have breakfast alone. He didn't mention it last night when we spoke on the phone. I grab my phone and text him a quick hello.

He responds almost immediately, asking how my day is going.

I'm typing my response when he walks into the boutique holding a to-go box from the diner. I pocket my phone. "I was just replying to your message."

"Hello again, Ben," Leslie says. "Don't even tell me you didn't finish your omelet. I ate the entire thing!"

"I did, too. I bought this one for Hailey." He hands me the container.

"You didn't have to buy me breakfast."

"I didn't. I bought you brunch. I'm sure you ate a slice of toast for breakfast," he whispers.

I feel my cheeks warm. "Well, that was very sweet of you. Thank you."

"I had a meeting with the owner of the diner and decided to stay and eat after it since I skipped breakfast."

"Is the diner looking for help?" I ask. I may not be at the boutique for much longer. Not that I see myself waiting tables. I'd probably spill all the food on myself.

"Yeah, they've never used a temp agency before, but they said they've had a lot of turnover lately and are looking for people to fill in when needed."

A customer walks in, and Leslie says, "I've got this. You two talk." She walks over to help the customer.

"She spent the entire meal talking about how great you are," Ben says.

"Really? Leslie?" I ask.

"Okay, no. I was the one who did that." He blushes.

I smile at him. "Well, that makes me much happier to hear."

He reaches for my hand, giving it a gentle squeeze. "How's the investigation coming along?"

"I hit another roadblock this morning. Ruby Redford confirmed that she and Jesse went into Simone's office because the delivery man arrived at that time, and Simone had to go sign for the package."

"You think Maxwell lied about Simone being dead when he got here?" Ben's gaze goes toward the back rooms.

"That or someone killed Simone seconds before Maxwell arrived with the package."

"You want to talk to Maxwell again to see if he remembers seeing anything, don't you?"

"Leslie and I were in the front of the store. Jesse and Ruby were in Simone's office. Laurent was in his office. That means the killer had to have been hiding in the storage room."

"If that's true, they were still there when the police arrived on the scene, but that's not possible."

He's right. But that leaves Maxwell, and I'm not willing to believe Pete's good friend is the murderer.

At six o'clock, Ben, Riley, and I show up at the police station unannounced. I figured surprising Detective Bilson was the best way to go. He clearly doesn't agree, because when he sees us, his entire body goes rigid. He ushers us into the conference room.

"What are you three doing here?"

"We need to talk to Maxwell Decker," I say.

"Hailey, I've spent my entire day grilling Laurent and Ivy Vincent about a flash drive they may or may not have in their possession. They've lawyered up and are threatening to press charges for harassment."

"That's absurd," Riley says. "This is a murder investigation. You have every right to question them."

"That's the problem. The lawyer doesn't see the will as part of the murder investigation, especially since it was a secret will no one but Simone knew the contents of."

I guess I did put him in a bad situation there. "Detective, I'm sorry. I just thought you should know what I overheard."

"I'm glad you told me, Hailey. It was the right thing to do."

"Wait. What?" Riley asks. "You're not going to yell at her?"

"For doing her civic duty and reporting something she thought could be important to an open investigation? Certainly not." With the way Detective Bilson is looking at Riley, I get the feeling he's trying to prove something to her.

"Detective, even if it's not connected to the murder, they still stole from Vance Brooks. Can't you run with that?"

"I'm trying to, but I haven't been able to get in contact with Vance Brooks."

Because he doesn't want the will to come to light either! If it doesn't, he gets everything because he's her spouse. I'm not the biggest fan of Simone, and I understand the family being upset if she did cut them out of her will. But at the same time, it was her money, and the woman is dead. Part of me thinks her dying wish should be granted.

"He wouldn't skip town," Riley says. "It would make him look guilty."

"I agree," Detective Bilson says. "So where is he?"

"Grieving?" Ben suggests. "We know Simone didn't love her husband all that much, but that doesn't mean the feeling was mutual."

Detective Bilson looks at Riley. "That I can believe. I don't know where he'd go to grieve, though."

"Probably somewhere that meant a lot to them when they were younger," Riley says. "You know…when they were in love." She looks away from Detective Bilson.

This is painful to watch. It's like they keep making these masked declarations of their feelings for each other. I want to shake them both.

"Detective, I really need to talk to Maxwell Decker."

"He's already told me everything he remembers from Monday."

"Who was the package from?" I ask. "The one Maxwell delivered on Monday when he found Simone's body."

Detective Bilson shrugs. "I'm not sure. I never thought to ask him. Why?"

"Maxwell said there were delivery instructions on it."

"Right, from Simone Vincent."

"No. How could it be from Simone? She didn't send the package."

"No, but she has all her deliveries marked with the keycode for the back door. Those instructions go on every package."

"But were they the only instructions?"

"What are you getting at, Hailey?"

"What if the killer sent the package so the delivery man would find the body?"

"You think Maxwell Decker was setup?" Detective Bilson asks.

"It's possible, right?"

"I guess so."

"So where is the package? We need to find it."

"It has to be in the storage room. I'm assuming Maxwell put it down when he picked up the murder weapon."

"Let's ask him and find out."

Detective Bilson looks at Riley. "I can't believe I'm going along with this, but why not?" He opens the door of the conference room. "The Vincents are in interrogation room one, so we'll use room two. Go sit. I'll get Maxwell."

We enter the room.

"I can't believe he's entertaining this," Riley says.

"I can."

Ben gives me a knowing look. He picked up the same things I did between Riley and Detective Bilson.

"I guess he's finally coming to his senses and realizing you're better at his job than he is." Riley smirks.

I really hope they aren't recording this room yet because that is the last thing Detective Bilson needs to hear Riley say if he watches the tapes.

He comes into the room with Maxwell in handcuffs.

"Hi, Maxwell," I say, taking a seat across from him.

"Do you have good news for me, Hailey?" he asks.

"I'm doing my best. I promise." I don't even care that my declaration is in front of Detective Bilson. I'm pretty sure he knows I never stopped investigating this murder.

"Maxwell, I need you to remember the moment you arrived at Belle Boutique."

"Okay."

"Did you see anyone leaving the parking lot?"

"No."

"Did you see anyone leaving the storage room either through the back door or into the boutique itself?"

"No." He looks down at his cuffed hands.

"So, when you arrived, you were carrying the package, right?"

"Yes."

"Did you see who it was from?"

"It was from a company. I think it was a package of display materials. You know signs and such for the shelves. I've seen the company logo before on things I've delivered to the boutique."

"What happened to that package?" Detective Bilson asks.

"I put it down by the door after I scanned it. We always leave the packages right inside the door. Unless there are already several there. Then we have to go inside the storage room more than usual."

"Okay, so the door chimed, and you announced your arrival because you needed a signature."

"No. There was no signature required for the delivery. And there was no door chime either."

"Are you certain?" I ask.

"I'm sure of it," Maxwell says. "I even remember thinking it must be broken because I've delivered packages there before and heard it every time but that one."

I turn to Detective Bilson. "You need to see if the chime is working. If it's not, anyone could have gotten into that storage room."

"You told me Ruby said she heard it, though," Ben says.

"That's true. She did say that."

"Is it possible she heard the register?" Detective Bilson asks.

"Leslie was counting the drawer, and the register does chime when the drawer opens. It's possible that's what Ruby heard," I say.

"That means someone could have snuck into the storage room, killed Simone, and left before Maxwell arrived with his delivery."

"Does this mean I'm off the hook?" Maxwell asks.

"Not so fast," Detective Bilson says. "It means I'm willing to believe someone else killed Simone Vincent."

Riley smiles at Detective Bilson.

I'm sure she's proud of him for being open-minded. I am, too, but our job is far from over. We still have no idea who snuck into the storage room and killed Simone.

CHAPTER TEN

Riley has a huge smile on her face as she pets Marley in her lap. "I still can't believe Garrett is looking into other suspects."

Ben leans back on the couch, his arm draped behind me. "I think he was trying to get your approval, Riley."

Riley flips a hand in the air. "He'd never do that. He just finally stopped being so pigheaded."

Speaking of being pigheaded… She's completely blind to what's going on between her and Garrett.

"I have an early meeting in the morning, and it's getting late," Ben says. "I should get going."

"I'll walk you to the door." I stand up with him.

"Good night, Ben," Riley says before winking at me.

I swat at her as I follow Ben to the door.

"How about lunch tomorrow? You don't have to work, right?"

"Actually, I have no idea. I wasn't originally on the schedule for Saturday, but with Jesse gone, it's possible Laurent will need me."

"You're sure he has no idea you're the one who told Detective Bilson about the flash drive and what you overheard him and his wife discussing?"

"I don't think he does." I haven't seen him since yesterday morning, though, so I can't say for certain. I'd assume Detective

Bilson would give me a heads-up if he thought the Vincents blamed me in any way for them being called into the station.

"Promise me you won't go into work then."

"If Leslie calls me in a panic to go help her out, I know I'll go. I'm just being honest with you."

He smiles. "I appreciate that, but call me first if that happens."

"What do you plan to do?" I ask with a smile.

"I've always wanted to play the part of the knight in shining armor."

"Is that so? Why do I think you've probably saved a few damsels in distress before?"

"Never. Women are tough. They rarely need saving."

My smile widens. "I like your answer."

"This is the longest goodbye ever," Riley calls from the living room. "Just kiss her already and be done with it."

"She's so romantic," I say.

"This could be why she's so oblivious to her own feelings for a certain detective," he whispers before leaning down to kiss me goodnight.

"See you tomorrow," I say, closing the door behind him.

"He did kiss you, right?" Hailey calls from the couch.

I walk back into the living room and sit down. "You know, you should take less interest in my dating life."

She holds up a hand in surrender. "I'm only trying to help."

"There's something I need to talk to you about." I look down at a string on the couch cushion.

"If it's about Garrett Bilson, consider the conversation already over."

"It is but not in the way you're thinking."

"This has nothing to do with feelings?" she asks.

"No. It has to do with Rumor Robin. He knows it's you."

She narrows her eyes at me. "How do you know this?"

"He followed me home last night and told me he knew you're behind the column. I never admitted to anything. He said I didn't have to, and he's glad I'm so loyal to you because you deserve to have someone look out for you that way. But he knows, Riles. He said you used to write for the school paper, and your writing style hasn't changed all that much from then. He also gave you credit for trying to throw him off your scent with some of the things you wrote about."

She leans back on the couch and huffs, getting a loud meow from Marley in the process. "I guess I knew he'd figure it out eventually. I can't believe the column is finished, though."

She can't give up the column because of this. There's no reason to. "He's not going to tell anyone. Your secret is perfectly safe with him.."

"I'm not sure I want to continue the column if he knows I'm behind it."

"If you don't, other people might figure out it was you."

"How?" she asks.

"What would you do at the paper? We both know you'd never really be your uncle's assistant even if that's your current cover story."

"No way." She puts her feet up on the couch, and Marley jumps down, annoyed that she won't stay in the position he wanted her in.

"I don't see you wanting to cover the news either," I say.

"Okay, I see your point. I just hate that he found out. I liked having one thing about myself that he didn't know."

There's another thing he doesn't know. A big thing. Her true feelings for him. "I'm sure you have other secrets. He knows you well, but you keep a lot from him, too."

"I don't think so, but I appreciate you saying it anyway. And thanks again for trying to cover for me and pretend you're Rumor Robin."

"That's what friends are for."

"Hey, Simone Vincent didn't have any friends, did she?"

"I think the only person she got along with was Ruby Redford. I mean Leslie was nice to her, but I think that was mostly out of fear."

"Fear can be a good motivator at times." Riley laughs. "Can you imagine if Leslie turns out to be the killer?"

"I was with her the whole time. It's not her."

"Too bad. I kind of like the *disgruntled employee offing her tyrant boss* angle."

"You're scaring me a little, considering your boss is your uncle."

"Uncle Sammy isn't a tyrant by any means. He's a big old teddy bear. To me at least."

"Is he not that way with the other employees?"

"Not all. I've found bosses are usually nice to two groups of people. Those they actually like, and those they pretend they like for their own benefit."

"People like Laurent because he's nice to everyone."

"I think he had to be because his sister was a royal pain in the butt. It's like the good cop, bad cop routine. You need balance."

"So you think he was just playing a part?"

"Maybe. He had access to the back room. His office is right next to it."

I swallow hard. "And he had no idea what was in her secret will at the time. He might have gotten so fed up with his sister that he killed her, snuck back into his office, and left the body for the deliveryman to find because he knew the delivery was coming that evening." It all lines up. "He even had an excuse for his fingerprints being on the murder weapon since the clothing rack is in his boutique. Of course, he's touched it."

Riley nods. "He makes more sense as the killer than anyone else if you ask me."

And I've been seeing glimpses of another side to Laurent Vincent since Simone's murder. Maybe it's bringing out his true colors.

Laurent Vincent could be the killer after all.

After talking to Ben in the morning and telling him the theory Riley and I came up with, he insists I don't step foot inside the boutique today. Okay, he didn't insist. He begged me not to. No part of me wants to be anywhere near Laurent right now, but I feel bad leaving Leslie on her own. She's been so scared all this time. The only time she's smiled since the murder is when she's around Ben.

Oh my goodness. I think she has a crush on my sort of, maybe boyfriend. Is it wrong that I suddenly feel less guilty for leaving her alone at the boutique after coming to that realization?

Yes! I know it is. I've seen plenty of women eye up Ben. You'd have to be completely oblivious to not notice how attractive the man is.

Leslie calls my phone at nine in the morning. "Hailey, tell me you're just running late."

"No, I'm not on the schedule today."

"But Jesse's gone. He's supposed to be working, but he skipped town, remember? I'm here all alone. I can't stay here alone. Laurent isn't even in. I'm scared, Hailey."

Since Detective Bilson wasn't able to locate Vance Brooks and get him to press charges against Laurent and Ivy Vincent, Laurent was free to go. I'm assuming he'll show up at the boutique at some point. I have a feeling he has that flash drive hidden here somewhere. "Leslie, breathe. Have you spoken to Laurent? Does he even know you're there?"

"No. I assumed you and I had to work because Jesse isn't on staff anymore."

"Okay, then here's what I want you to do. Grab your purse, walk out the door, and lock it behind you."

"I can't do that! I'll get fired."

"Leslie, you're a good worker. You'll find another job. Ben can even help you if you'd like, but you need to leave the boutique."

"You're afraid of Laurent," she says. "You think he killed Simone. Oh my goodness. You're right. It has to be him. You and I were together. And Jesse and Ruby were together. If it wasn't the deliveryman, then Laurent is the only one left." Her voice is high-pitched and squeaky.

"Leslie, did you leave yet?"

"I can't move. I'm frozen in fear, Hailey."

"Keep talking to me. You're going to be okay. Take one step toward the door. You can do it."

"One step. Okay. I'm going." She gets quiet for a moment and then squeals. "I can't do it. I can't move, Hailey."

If she doesn't calm down, she's going to hyperventilate. "Leslie, breathe. Listen to me. Look out the front windows. Do you see Pete Modell?"

"No. I don't see him."

"I'm going to call him and have him come get you."

"No, don't get off the phone with me."

I move toward the front door. By the time I get to the boutique, Laurent might already be there. But I can't stand here and do nothing while Leslie has a nervous breakdown. "I'm on my way."

"Oh, thank you, Hailey."

"Stay on the phone, and keep trying to move toward the door." I get in my car and back out of the driveway. I put my phone on speaker in the middle console as I drive. "Talk loudly, Leslie. I had to put you on speaker so I can drive."

"Don't you have Bluetooth?" she asks.

My car is way too old for that, and it's a base model since that's all I could afford. I have exactly zero bells and whistles in this vehicle.

"No, I don't. Just keep talking." I try not to let my frustration show in my tone.

"Okay, I'm going to take a step now."

"Good."

There's a shuffling on the other end of the line. "I did it!"

"Great. Take another." I'm still five minutes away. Hopefully, Leslie can get herself out of the store before I arrive.

"I'm doing it. Wait. No. I forgot my purse. It's still behind the counter. I have to go back."

I always criticized the way screenwriters have victims in horror movies act when they're being pursued by killers, but Leslie is like a living, breathing embodiment of every single one of those victims rolled into one.

"Leslie, you need to hurry."

"Okay, I got my purse. I just have to get back to the door now."

"Go. As fast as you can."

"Hailey." This time her voice is a whisper.

"What is it?" I can't even imagine what's happening now. Did she trip over air and break her leg? That would be fitting.

"Laurent is here. He just pulled up directly in front of the store. I'm trapped." Her voice is still barely a whisper.

"Leslie, look for Pete. Do you see him outside?" I step down harder on the gas pedal. I need to get to her now.

"I don't see him. Hailey…" Sobs take over the rest of her sentence.

"Leslie, listen to me. You need to act natural. If Laurent thinks you know something or you're afraid of him, it will only make things worse. You need to be your usual bubbly self. Can you do that?"

"I don't think so. I'm so scared."

"I know you are, but I know you can do this. Be strong, Leslie. Wipe your face, and put on a smile when he walks in."

"I don't want to get off the phone."

"Don't. Tell him you're talking to me, and I'm on my way in. Tell him I called you because I had car trouble and wanted to let you know I was going to be late."

"Okay. He's coming inside now," she says. "How far away are you?" she asks in a much cheerier voice. At least she's doing her best to pull off the ruse.

"I'm about two minutes from you."

"Good. Oh, Laurent just got here. Good morning, Laurent. I'll get your coffee in a moment. I have Hailey on the phone. She ran into some car trouble and was calling to let us know she's running late. Wasn't that so thoughtful and responsible of her? She's such a great employee. I'm so happy she joined our little family here at Belle Boutique."

Wow! That was way over the top, but Leslie must be the type to ramble when she's nervous.

"I hope everything's okay," I hear Laurent say in the background. "I'll be in my office. Come back once Hailey is here."

"Sure thing," Leslie says.

I pull up to the boutique. "Leslie, I'm here. I have to hang up and make another phone call. Do you see me through the window?" I wave to get her attention, and she waves back.

"Yes. Hurry."

I end the call and dial Ben.

"Good morning," he says.

"I'm at the boutique. Leslie called me in a panic. She was in tears, and Laurent showed up. I had to come in."

"I'll be right there." I hear a rustling on the other end of the line and know he's on his way.

I get out of the car and walk into the boutique, remaining near the door.

Leslie's eyes widen at me, and she mouths, "He's in his office."

I nod in response and motion for her to come toward me. Now that I'm here, she's able to move again.

"Leslie," Laurent says, walking back into the boutique. He looks up when he sees us by the door. "Oh, Hailey, good. You're exactly the person I need to speak to."

"Me?" I ask, unsure why he'd want to talk to me, unless he still suspects I was in his office yesterday.

"Yes, can you come to my office please?" He looks at Leslie. "My coffee can wait."

Is that code for don't interrupt us? Is he planning to kill me and then Leslie before making a run for it?

CHAPTER ELEVEN

Leslie hasn't moved, and she's looking at me as if I have the answers to solving this dilemma. I'm not liking the idea of going into Laurent's office with him alone one bit. I have to get out of here, but I can't leave Leslie either.

"Um, I'll be right there, Laurent. I need to grab something from my car. I asked Leslie to help me because it's heavy." I'm making this up as I go, and the worst part is I have no idea what I could possibly be retrieving from my car if he questions me about it.

"Is everything all right?" he asks.

"Not really. I had some car trouble, and the guy who stopped to help me fix the car said I needed to get a part from the store. I have to go get it to read the part number off of, but it's heavy, like I said." The only thing I can come up with to remove would be the battery, and I doubt it would take both Leslie and me to carry one.

"I can help you if you need," Laurent says.

This is getting worse by the second. I look out the front window and see Ben's Silverado pull up. "Oh, there's Ben now. He said he'd meet me here to help out. I'm sure he can get it for me. I don't want you to get your nice shirt dirty anyway. You know how greasy car parts can be." I give a nervous laugh.

"Okay, then I guess I will take that coffee while I wait for Hailey, Leslie. Could you get on that?"

Now I've put Leslie back in harm's way, which wasn't my intention at all.

Ben walks in, and I relax a little having him here. He immediately walks over to me and places a hand on my back. "You all right, Hailey?" His voice is strained, like he's trying to keep it together and not lash out at my boss, who may or may not be a coldblooded killer.

"Just a little rattled over the car thing this morning," I say. "Oh, Leslie, can I get the number for the mechanic you use before you go get Laurent's coffee? You said you have your last service paper in your glove compartment, right? In your car?" I hope it's not glaringly obvious that I'm leading her into this response.

"Oh, yes! In my car. I'll go grab it for you now." She hurries past Ben and me, right out the door.

"Good thinking," Ben says as we follow her out.

Laurent has a look of total confusion on his face as he watches us all leave.

"I can't believe that worked," I say.

"You're so smart, Hailey," Leslie says. "I was too terrified to think."

"You did great."

"Can I go home now?" she asks as if she needs my permission.

"I'll tell Laurent you weren't feeling well. Go." I give her arm a gentle tap.

"Thank you. Both of you." She nods to us before getting into her car and driving away.

Luckily, Laurent isn't watching us anymore. He must have gone back into his office.

"What now?" I ask Ben.

"You can't go to work."

"Someone has to keep an eye on Laurent."

Ben tilts my head up so I'm looking into his eyes. "That's Detective Bilson's job. Not yours."

"Right because my job is working in the boutique." I dip my head in the direction of the shop.

"Tell Laurent the mechanic needs you to come in now."

I guess that could work, and it would force Laurent to either close the boutique or work the register and showroom himself. He wouldn't be able to engage in any illegal activities out in the open like that. "I'll go tell him."

"I'm going with you."

I was expecting him to say that.

We walk back into the boutique and right to Laurent's office. He's on the phone by the sound of it. I pause to listen before knocking.

"I can't. There's no point anyway. Ivy already gave you the flash drive." There's a moment of silence, and then he says, "I don't care what that detective told you. Believe what you want." There's a loud bang, like he slammed his phone down on his desk. He must have been talking to Vance Brooks. Detective Bilson couldn't get ahold of him, but he clearly left a message telling him his suspicions about the flash drive. And it sounds like Vance discovered Detective Bilson was right about Ivy switching the flash drives. Now Vance wants the real one back.

I raise my hand and knock on the door.

"Come in," Laurent barks, which is so out of character for his usually very composed demeanor. Maybe all of this is finally getting to him.

I open the door. "I'm sorry if I'm interrupting something," I say.

"No, Hailey, you're fine. Come in." He finally looks up at me and sees Ben. "Mr. Traum, what can I do for you?"

"Ben's actually here for me. The mechanic needs me to bring my car in right away. He's booked solid and can only take me if I go right now. I'm really sorry, but seeing as I'm not actually on the schedule to work today anyway, I'm hoping you'll understand."

"Yes, sure. We'll talk when you're finished at the mechanic. Would you please send Leslie in? She still hasn't gotten my coffee."

It's interesting how Laurent is becoming more like Simone now that she's dead. He didn't strike me as the type to ask his employees to get him coffee.

"Leslie went home. She wasn't feeling well, and I think she might have a fever. She asked me to tell you."

"So I have no one to run the boutique?" he asks.

I can't help thinking he really was fooling us all with his nice guy act.

"Would you like me to put the closed sign on the front door on my way out?"

He huffs. "I guess so. I have so much paperwork to tend to here I can't possibly run the store myself." He waves a hand in the air.

"I'll do that then." I push Ben out of the office and close the door behind us.

"How long before Vance Brooks shows up here to confront his brother-in-law?" Ben asks.

"Probably not long, which is why Laurent doesn't want to be visible through the front window. He's going to hide from Vance for as long as possible."

We walk out to my car.

"What do we do?" I ask Ben.

"Well, we have to move your car in case Laurent does come out of his office. So let's take it to Riley's place and leave it there. I'll drive us after that."

I nod and get into my car. Ben follows me to Riley's. She comes out when she sees us pull up.

"What are you both doing here?"

"Stashing my car, which is supposed to be at the mechanic as far as Laurent Vincent is concerned." I quickly fill her in.

"Wow. So you think Laurent really did kill his sister."

"The pieces of the puzzle seem to fit," I say. "Want to come with us? We're going to stake out the boutique to see what Laurent does."

"Sure. I have no plans, and Marley has already decided he's had enough of my company. He went upstairs to bed."

She locks her door, and we all get into Ben's truck.

"You know, I'm a little worried about the author of the Rumor Robin column," Ben says.

"Why?" Riley asks.

"Well, she's the one who outed the whole business with Simone's will. Don't you think Laurent or one of the other family members would be angry with her for that?"

"What makes you so certain Rumor Robin is a woman?" Riley asks.

"I'm not. There are plenty of people Rumor Robin could possibly be. Your uncle for one. It's his paper. He knows everything that goes on in town, and I'm sure you feed him information as well." Ben looks at Riley in the rearview mirror.

"I will neither confirm or deny that accusation." She crosses her arms.

"She totally does," I say, hoping it will protect her true identity. I feel bad about keeping this secret from Ben, but it's not mine to tell. Riley clearly likes and trusts Ben, but she has to be the one to tell him the truth.

"All right, who else do you suspect?" Riley asks Ben.

"Pete Modell is the prime suspect, but if it is him, your uncle was filling in while Pete was gone." Ben's brow furrows. "Unless…" He pulls into a parking space across the street from Belle Boutique and turns to face Riley. "Did *you* fill in for Pete while he was away doing community service?"

"Me? Why do think I did that?"

"Come on, Riles. You have to know who Rumor Robin is. I'm sure your uncle wants you to keep it a secret, but I know you know."

She bobs one shoulder. "Maybe I do. Maybe I don't."

"I have to be right. It's either your uncle or Pete. It just makes sense. And you probably help them get their information."

"Look who thinks he's a detective," Riley says.

"I think we should be focusing on this murder investigation," I say, trying to change the topic. "How do we find out if Laurent gets to keep all the money in the business's name now that Simone is dead?"

"We'd need to talk to his lawyer and maybe the bank manager, too," Riley says. "But they'd never discuss confidential client information like that with us, so it would be a complete waste of time."

"Then what can we do?" Ben asks.

"Not even Detective Bilson would be able to get that information because Vance Brooks isn't pressing charges for theft of the flash drive," I say.

"Not yet at least." Riley leans forward in her seat. "But maybe we could persuade him to."

"How?" Ben asks.

"Come on. I can't think of everything," Riley says, resting an arm on the back of my seat. "Think, Hailey."

"I could tell Vance what I overheard Laurent and Ivy discussing. That might be enough to make him go to the police. But the problem is that the will screwed over Vance as well. He's not going to benefit from getting it back."

Ben nods. "Right, which means he might let the whole thing drop and just fight Laurent in court over the money from the business that was technically Simone's half."

"Then we have nothing to sway him with," I say. Nothing but the prospect that Laurent might have killed Simone. "Do we really believe Vance loved Simone?" I ask them both.

"I think he did," Ben says.

"Yeah, I kind of agree." Riley leans her head on my seat. "But what does that matter now?"

"If we can convince Vance that Laurent had reason to kill Simone, Vance might confront him to find out for sure."

"There is another option," Riley says, and the pure look of evil genius on her face makes me really nervous.

"What are you up to?" I ask.

"Well, if one of us pretends to be Simone's lawyer and goes to the family with a will Simone left in our confidence—"

"Hang on," Ben says. "That would never work. Everyone in town knows you, Riley. And Hailey and I work with Laurent. No one would believe any of us were lawyers."

"Then we hire someone to play the part."

"Hire someone to try to con a wealthy family that could turn around and sue this poor, unsuspecting wannabe actor for everything they have?" I pause and wait for her to see how crazy her plan actually is.

"Okay, but at least admit it would have been epic to watch."

"But this isn't a TV sitcom. It's real life, and someone close to Simone murdered her." I'm convinced it's someone she didn't see as a threat, which is why she never yelled or tried to call for help. She was comfortable being in that storage room with the killer because she never suspected their true intentions. This person fooled her, and they're clearly fooling us as well.

"I'm going to try contacting Vance Brooks," I say. "Maybe I can convince him to question his brother-in-law about Simone's murder."

I grab my phone and look up Brooks's number. It's not difficult to find, though I suspect it's his landline and not his cell phone. I'm even more convinced of it when it keeps ringing and ringing. "Not even an answering machine," I say, ending the call.

"Let me try to get his cell phone number," Riley says. She types something into her phone and then puts it in her lap.

"You just texted Detective Bilson, didn't you?"

"Garrett's our best shot. We know he has Vance's number." Her gaze volleys between Ben and me. "Why are you both looking at me like that?"

"No reason," I say, and I have to repress a smile.

"I believe in using all your resources to the best of your advantage." Her phone chimes with a text, and when she reads it, she rolls her eyes. "Why can't he ever just do what I ask? He has to hit me with a million questions first." She's furiously typing away a response.

"Don't anger him, or he'll never help us."

"He's a thorn in my side." She drops the phone in her lap after she sends the message.

"What did you say?" I ask, afraid she lost any hope of getting Detective Bilson's help.

"Don't worry about it."

Her phone chimes again, and this time I grab it before she can.

"Give that back!" She reaches for the phone, but I yank it away, positioning it between me and the door where she can't reach. "You threatened to tell everyone he wet the bed until he was ten! Riley!"

"What? It's not like I'd be lying." She crosses her arms. "What did he say? Did he give in?"

"He said he had a bladder infection."

She scoffs. "Likely story."

"He also said he'd text me with Vance's number." Right on cue, my own phone gets a notification. I toss Riley's phone back to her. "Got it." I press on the number to dial it. After three rings, it goes to voice mail. Vance must not answer calls from unfamiliar numbers. I can't blame him. No one wants to talk to telemarketers. After the beep, I leave a message. "Mr. Brooks, this is Hailey Hart. I feel weird about calling to tell you this, but I overheard something yesterday. Laurent and his wife were in his office, and they were talking about Simone's will. I didn't hear everything, but the way they were acting scared me. I think they might have had something to do with Simone's death. It's so scary to think I might be working for a murderer, but Laurent was in his office when Simone died. Or he said he was. He easily could have killed her and then hid in his office until the body was discovered. I thought you had a right to know. She was your wife after all." I hang up.

"Good job, Hailey. You sounded both scared and convincing." Riley pats my shoulder. "Just never take my phone like that again."

I text Detective Bilson back to thank him. Instead of responding, he calls me.

"What are you up to?" he asks me.

"I left a message for Vance, telling him I suspect Laurent might have killed Simone."

"Are you crazy? If I thought that was what you were doing, I never would have given you his number. I thought you were trying to help me track him down."

"He never went anywhere. I heard him on the phone with Laurent a little bit ago. They were arguing about the flash drive."

"So he's hiding out at home." Detective Bilson gets quiet. "Why would he be avoiding me?"

"I don't know. Maybe he's trying to figure out what happened to his wife. Or maybe he was hoping you'd let the matter of Simone's will drop if you couldn't get ahold of him."

"I have no proof that Simone Vincent had a secret will, so it's not like I can force anyone to hand over that flash drive," Detective Bilson says.

"And without it, you're lacking motive for the murder."

"If the two are actually connected to begin with," he says. "I'm sending CSI back to dust the back door for prints and check out the chime that's supposed to go off when someone opens the door from the outside. If I can find evidence it was tampered with, then I can at least entertain the theory that someone setup Maxwell Decker to take the fall for the murder."

"Who else knew that the delivery was being made on Monday?" I ask.

"Only the company who sent it, Maxwell Decker, Simone, and Laurent Vincent." He pauses. "Unless Simone informed the employees of expected deliveries."

"She didn't tell me, but she might have mentioned it to either Leslie or Jesse."

"Jesse Merrill hasn't returned to town yet," Detective Bilson says. "I spoke to his mother about twenty minutes ago."

"You think that makes him look guilty."

"A little, yeah. Was he ever out of your sight?"

"Yeah, I can't place his whereabouts at all times the way I can with Leslie's."

"So he should remain on my suspect list."

"I guess so." I feel bad for saying that since Jesse is only eighteen and not here to defend himself. But running away at a time like this does look suspicious.

"Okay, I have work to do. If you hear from Vance Brooks, I want to know immediately."

"You got it," I tell him before hanging up.

"Hailey, look." Riley points across the street. "Laurent is leaving the boutique."

I turn to Ben. "You need to follow him."

"You want me to tail him? He knows my truck, and you and I are supposed to be at the mechanic."

"Then don't be seen," I say, realizing I'm asking him to do the nearly impossible.

CHAPTER TWELVE

To my surprise, Laurent pulls into the funeral home. I didn't even stop to think that there would be services for Simone Vincent. How did I forget about that? The police arrested Maxwell Decker. The only one who thinks there might be other leads to track down is Detective Bilson, and that's because Riley, Ben, and I made him consider that possibility. Everyone else at the station is happy to pin the murder on Maxwell Decker.

I immediately call Detective Bilson. "Did you know the services for Simone Vincent are going on right now?"

"No. They were never publicized."

Then it must be a family-only kind of service. "Do you think the family is trying to cover up something by keeping the public away?"

"Which funeral home at you at?" Detective Bilson asks.

"The one on Mulberry."

"I'm on my way. Don't do anything without me." He hangs up before I can respond.

"We can't just sit in the truck and do nothing," Riley says.

"If it's really a closed service, we won't be let inside," Ben says. "Our best bet is to wait for Detective Bilson to get here and try to go inside with him."

"You think Garrett Bilson will have better luck getting inside than we will?" Riley scoffs. "Please. We can totally do this."

"How exactly?" These people know our faces. We can't walk right in there pretending to be long-lost family. Besides, long lost family wouldn't even know about the service.

Riley turns to me and smiles. "I have an idea. Anyone have a flash drive on them?"

"No." I turn in my seat to face her. "Why?"

"What if we create a new fake will and tell everyone Simone gave it to you and asked you to hold on to it. You can pretend she suspected someone was trying to kill her, and you were her backup plan to make her secret will publicly known at her funeral service."

Who gives a complete stranger something as personal as their last will and testament? "I'd think she'd entrust something like that to Leslie or Jesse before the employee she hired the same day she was killed."

"People do crazy and irrational things all the time," Riley says. "But for this plan to work, we need a flash drive."

"No, we don't," Ben says. "We just need an online will and access to it."

"This has to be completely illegal," I say. I'm not looking to get arrested today. It will be pretty tough to clear Maxwell Decker's name if I'm sharing a jail cell with the man.

"Okay, then we don't fake a will. We send the family on a wild goose chase to find it." Riley leans forward. "Let's come up with a riddle or something that they have to try to solve."

"What have you been watching on TV?" I ask her.

"Too much?"

Ben and I both nod.

Riley throws her hands in the air. "I don't hear either of you coming up with a plan."

I lean my head back on the seat, unable to think of a way to get inside that funeral home without Detective Bilson's help. I'm about to give up when I see someone walk up to the front door of the funeral home. "Who is that?" I ask, sitting up straighter. "I've seen him before."

"You have?" Riley asks. "That's Erik Sinclair. Where do you know him from?"

"He was at the boutique on Monday. He came to see Simone, but Laurent lied to him and said Simone wasn't available."

"Simone was avoiding him, then, and Laurent knew about it," Ben says.

"Yeah, I think so. Who is Erik Sinclair anyway?"

"He's a wannabe designer. His day job is with some company that stocks supplies for small businesses, but he wants to be a designer one day," Riley says.

"How do you know that?" Ben asks her.

"Pete Modell told me. He said Erik delivers a lot of supplies to the local businesses, so he sees him a lot. Erik mentioned how he wants to start his own clothing line one day, and his current job is just to pay the bills until his fashion dream becomes a reality.

"Hold up," I say. "He works for a company that delivers supplies to local businesses?"

"Yeah, I don't remember the name of the company, though."

"But it very well could be the company that Maxwell was delivering the package from on Monday evening." If it was, that can't be a coincidence, can it?

"Why wouldn't Erik deliver it himself?" Riley asks. "If that's his job, it would only make sense."

"I don't think he was working on Monday. He came in to meet with Simone. He wouldn't have been able to if he was working that day."

"So he had the day off but easily could have known about the delivery," Ben says, reading my mind.

"Exactly. And he was angry with Simone when I saw him."

"Angry enough to have killed her?" Ben asks.

"I don't know him well enough to say."

"Well, he doesn't appear to be getting inside the funeral home," Riley says, pointing to the door where a man working security is pushing Erik Sinclair away from the door.

"Let's go see what's going on." I get out of the truck and hurry over to them. "Mr. Sinclair?" I call. "Is that you?"

He turns to look at me, and it's clear he doesn't recognize me from our brief encounter on Monday. "Do I know you?"

I figure I can play this to my advantage. "No, but I know you. I've seen some of your designs."

"You have?" He furrows his brow at me, and then his gaze raises to Ben and Riley coming up behind me. "Where?"

I think fast. "In Simone's office. I work at the boutique."

"Wait." He holds up a hand. "You've seen my work in Simone's office?"

"Yes. I loved it and asked her whose it was."

"And she actually gave you my name?"

"Well, no. Leslie did. The girl who works the register," I add in case he doesn't know Leslie by name.

"I don't know why Simone would have my designs in her office. She turned me down and told me my designs were too commonplace for her boutique."

"You're kidding me." I press a hand to my chest, feigning disbelief. "Your designs are so cutting edge." I'm not even sure I know what that means in the fashion world, but I'm hoping he'll buy it.

"When did you see the designs?" he asks.

"On Monday. It was after you came in to see her."

"But I didn't get to see her. She hid from me and made Laurent get rid of me."

"How do you know she did that?" I ask, turning slightly as a breeze tries to blow my hair in my face.

"I'm sure that's what happened. I met with her Sunday. She told me to get lost because she was never going to sell my designs in her store. I went back on Monday, hoping to reason with her after she'd had time to reconsider, but I'm sure she told her brother all about our argument the day before."

"Did this argument take place in the boutique?"

"Yeah, of course. I'm not crazy. I wouldn't show up at her house or something like that. You hear these horror stories about designers cornering big names in the business while they're in the bathroom or late at night in their own homes. I'd never resort to that. I'm not desperate. I know my designs are good. If the Vincents don't want to showcase them for me, I'll find someone else who will."

"Then why are you here for the funeral?" Riley asks him. "I can't imagine you liked Simone enough to come pay your respects."

Nor do I think the family extended an invite to him.

"I've been trying to get ahold of Laurent." He looks down at his shiny black shoes.

So he won't corner a seller in a bathroom, but he will try to corner one at his sister's funeral. Classy.

"I figured if I played nice and came to pay my respects, Laurent might reconsider working with me."

"Ever think to send flowers instead?" Riley asks.

"Oh, I did. They should be inside."

He's trying to capitalize on Simone's murder. A murder he stood to benefit from. "Mr. Sinclair, you had Monday off from your other job, didn't you?" I ask him.

"How do you know where I work?" He narrows his eyes at me.

"I told her," Riley says. "I know everything that goes on in this town."

Erik shakes a finger at Riley. "You're Riley Jacobs. I thought I knew you from somewhere."

"That's right. Most people in town know who I am."

"Your dad or someone owns the newspaper, right?"

"Uncle," she clarifies.

"That's why you think you know everything that goes on in town." He smirks. "How about asking your uncle to run a feature on my designs? I'd be happy to give him an exclusive."

"I could talk to him about it. What's it worth to you?" She crosses her arms in front of her chest.

"What do you want?"

"Answers. Where were you Monday evening around six o'clock?"

"Why—" He pauses. "Oh, I see. You all think I killed Simone because she wouldn't work with me."

"Did you?" Riley asks.

"No. I'd never throw my career away for Simone Vincent."

"But you did stand to gain from her death," I say. "Clearly you realize that or you wouldn't be trying to get on Laurent's good side."

"Yeah, so maybe I do. I'm sure others do as well."

"Like who?" I ask.

"Other designers. Simone paid them virtually nothing. She thought they should be grateful she was even putting their work in her boutique. She thought the exposure was the best form of payment."

"Are you saying the other designers weren't happy with Simone?" I ask.

"I highly doubt they were," he says.

"Then why did you want your work to be sold in Belle Boutique?" I ask.

"I'm sure you know what Simone was able to do for Ruby Redford. I figured Simone could get my name out there like that, and then I'd leave."

He planned to use Simone. Really nice.

"Did you know about the package being delivered to Belle Boutique Monday evening?" I ask.

"Like I said, I don't work on Mondays, so I wouldn't know anything about a package being delivered since I wasn't there."

I bob my head. "Well, thank you for talking to us, Mr. Sinclair. I hope you find a suitable place to showcase your designs."

He shoves his hands in his pockets and walks away.

"Why did you just let him go like that?" Riley asks me as Detective Bilson pulls up in his patrol car.

"What did I miss?" he asks as he jogs over to us.

"Hailey just let a perfectly good suspect go," Riley says.

"Riles, didn't you hear what he said?"

She shakes her head at me.

"He said if the delivery on Monday came from his company, he wouldn't know about it because he didn't work that day."

"Yeah, so?"

"So, we never told him the delivery came from *his* company," I say.

Detective Bilson points to me. "You got him to slip up and reveal he really did know about the delivery."

I smile and nod. "I did. And I think we should keep close tabs on Erik Sinclair."

CHAPTER THIRTEEN

Detective Bilson looks across the parking lot. "Did you see which way Erik Sinclair went when he left?"

I didn't consider letting him go meant losing him for the time being. I was just happy to have gotten more out of him than he realized. "Sorry, but no."

"All right, well, I can't be here at the funeral home *and* follow Sinclair. If you think Sinclair really slipped up about that delivery, then I'm willing to bet he's the more likely suspect at the moment. I'll try to track him down."

"Are you giving us permission to follow the family while you go after Sinclair?" Riley asks him.

"I never said that, but I can't be in two places at once." He winks at Riley. Like actually winks, and dare I say her cheeks get the slightest bit rosy? He backs away a few steps before turning and jogging to his patrol car.

Riley looks at me, and I wink, which makes her swat at my arm. "Knock it off. It was code, not flirting."

"Looked like flirting to me," Ben says.

Riley hits *his* arm this time. "Don't you start, too. Garrett was trying to let us know he wants us to watch the family so he can pursue Sinclair."

The wind starts kicking up, and I wrap my arms around myself.

"Let's go sit in the truck," Ben says. "It will look less suspicious than us standing around in the middle of the parking lot anyway."

We get back into the truck, and I lean against the door so I'm facing both Riley and Ben. "This case has so many different sides to it."

"You mean because there's the battle over the will, Simone's murder, and the possible issues between Simone and her designers?" Ben asks.

"Yeah, and don't forget about Jesse Merrill running away from home."

"It's almost like the actual murder is taking a back seat to all the other drama," Riley says.

"I wonder if the killer knew it would. I mean let's say it is Erik Sinclair. He clearly knew about the delivery that day, so he could count on Maxwell finding Simone's body. He also knew the other designers were being under paid by Simone. The question is, did Erik know about Simone's family issues as well?" I don't think he'd know she had a secret will, but if Simone didn't get along with her brother and was having trouble with her husband, that might have been obvious to Erik. He easily could have overheard something or even witnessed an altercation in person.

Riley bobs her head. "And for argument sake, let's say it's not Erik Sinclair. If Laurent killed his sister, he knew that Sinclair had argued with Simone the day before. And he must have also known the other designers were being under paid."

"Laurent had the contracts for the designers all over his desk," I say. "I saw them. He must have been going through them, which means he had to have been aware that there was trouble there."

"Trouble he could have used to keep suspicion off himself if the police didn't buy into Maxwell Decker being the killer," Ben adds.

"Wait. Did we just make cases against multiple people?" Riley asks.

"We did." I let out a deep sigh. "So if all these people could have killed Simone and had reason to, who actually went through with it?"

"That's the million-dollar question, Hails." Riley places her hand on my shoulder.

The services for Simone last for about two hours. I can only imagine what's going on inside that funeral home. I highly doubt they're exchanging happy memories of Simone. It's more likely the family is discussing Simone's money and whether or not there was ever a secret will. I'm dying to know if Laurent and Ivy are pretending to not have the will.

By the time they start to trickle out, my eyes can barely stay open. Ben gently nudges me when Vance Brooks comes out of the funeral home. He looks upset, but I can't tell if it's from anger or grief. Probably both. After Vance, Ivy walks out. I'm surprised she's not with Laurent. He must be here. She gets in her car and leaves on her own. We wait and wait.

"Where's Laurent?" Riley asks, voicing the question on my mind.

"Maybe he's talking to the funeral director."

"I'd think Vance would be the one to do that since he was Simone's husband," she says.

I've given up thinking anything this family does is what you'd expect from normal people.

"Do we keep waiting?" Ben asks.

"At least for a little longer," I say. I'm convinced he has to be here. It only makes sense that he would be. Maybe he and Ivy drove separately because Laurent was working. She might have been making other arrangements as well. I could speculate until I'm blue in the face.

The door opens, and Ruby Redford walks out with Laurent.

"What is she doing at a family-only service?" Riley asks.

"Apparently, Ruby was Simone's only real friend," I say. "She's also the biggest designer Simone and Laurent work with. He probably invited her because he's afraid of losing her now that Simone is gone."

"Nice. He's conducting business at his sister's funeral service."

"Shouldn't they all be going to the cemetery?" Ben asks.

"Not if Simone was cremated," Riley says. "Though I didn't see anyone leave with an urn."

"Do you want me to follow Laurent?" Ben asks, starting the engine.

"Yeah, let's stay with him." It's basically what we told Detective Bilson we'd do.

Laurent hugs Ruby goodbye after walking her to her car. Then he gets on his phone as he walks to his own vehicle.

"Who do you think he's calling?" Riley asks.

"Beats me." No sooner do the words leave my mouth than my phone rings, making me jump. I look at the screen. "It's Laurent."

"Don't answer it," Ben says.

He's right. I shouldn't answer. I can't let him know I'm not at the mechanic's, and since there are no sounds of cars being worked on in Ben's truck, it would be a dead giveaway. I wait for the call to go to voice mail.

Laurent is driving out of the parking lot now, and Ben keeps a safe distance as he follows. Once the voice mail alert chimes, I play it on speaker so everyone can hear.

"Hailey, it's Laurent. I hope your car is almost ready because I really need you at the boutique. Call me as soon as you get this."

"What could be so urgent?" Riley asks. "I get that Saturday is probably the boutique's busiest day, but in the midst of his sister's funeral, how much can he really care about being closed for the day?"

"How much longer do you think I can stall with the car trouble excuse? I'm not sure I could have an issue that would take this long to repair."

"You can always say they didn't have the right parts and had to go get them," Ben suggests. "That would take time."

Riley pats him on the shoulder. "You're handy to have around."

"Okay, that works for me, but it looks like Laurent is going back to the boutique. The only way for me to keep an eye on him is to go to work."

Riley leans forward in her seat. "Is that Vance?"

Sure enough, Vance Brooks is standing in front of the boutique, looking all around.

"Laurent may not be going to work after all," Ben says. "I doubt Vance confronted Laurent at the funeral service, but that's clearly what he intends to do here. Laurent will probably drive right by."

We slow down and watch. Laurent does drive by, but he puts on his blinker.

"He's going around to the back of the boutique," I say.

"I thought the back door was off-limits," Riley says.

"It is, but he used it at least once that I know of already."

I grab my phone and call Detective Bilson as Ben drives around to the back of the boutique.

"Bilson," he answers.

"We followed Laurent to the store. He's going in the back storage room."

"He's tampering with my crime scene!" Detective Bilson's sirens blare through the phone. "I'll be right there. Do not go inside."

The call ends.

The back door keeps opening and closing.

"What is he doing?" Riley asks.

"I think he's messing with the door alarm, the one that is supposed to chime to announce the deliverymen."

"How did he even know it wasn't working?" Ben asks.

He'd know if he was the one to disable it. I raise my phone and video what we're seeing.

Detective Bilson pulls into the lot about a minute later and goes right for the back door. He puts on a latex glove before he reaches the door, but as he's trying to open it, it swings out toward him, and he staggers backward.

"Please tell me you got that on tape, too," Riley says with a snicker.

I stop recording. I wish I could trim the video before Detective Bilson sees it and hears Riley's comment, but I'm not sure how to do that or if I even can from my phone.

Detective Bilson grabs Laurent and pulls him out of the boutique. We step out of the truck and head over to them.

"What do you think you're doing?" Laurent asks. "This is my boutique."

"This is my crime scene, and you're tampering with it, which is a crime I might add."

"I didn't tamper with anything."

"What exactly were you doing?" Detective Bilson asks.

"He was reactivating the back door chime," I say.

"Hailey." Laurent looks up at me.

"You knew the chime was disabled," I say, leveling him with a look. The only way you could have known that is if you're the one who disabled it."

"I knew because when I just opened the door, it didn't chime." Laurent narrows his eyes at me. "How did you know the alarm was disabled?"

"Maxwell Decker told the police the door didn't make a sound when he arrived with that package. He called for Simone to tell her."

"I have to wonder how you didn't hear him calling," Detective Bilson says to Laurent. "Your office is right next to the storage room."

"I was on a work call. You can check my phone records."

"I will. Now tell me what you think you were doing using this door. I can't imagine you somehow missed all the police tape."

"I left something in my office."

"The flash drive with Simone's secret will?" I ask.

Laurent glares at me. "Were you in my office?"

"I heard you and Ivy talking about it. I know you have the flash drive." I have a lot more confidence now that Detective Bilson has Laurent in handcuffs.

"You misunderstood us."

"Really? You weren't discussing how Simone left all her money to her own clothing line, cutting you and her husband completely out of her will?" I step toward him. "You and Ivy didn't speculate that Ruby was probably helping Simone pull all this off because Ruby was the only one Simone was close to?"

Laurent sighs.

"I think we should all head to the station and have a long talk," Detective Bilson says. He nods to me as he brings Laurent to the back of his patrol car.

"I think you're growing on him," Ben says.

"Garrett should be kissing Hailey's feet after all the help she's given him," Riley says on the drive.

"Let's not go that far." And if he's going to be kissing anyone, it's not going to be me. It's going to be a certain brunette in the back seat.

When we arrive at the station, Detective Bilson waves us to an interrogation room.

"Were you able to track down Erik Sinclair?" I ask.

"No. I went to his place of business, and found his car but not him. I was informed he's out making deliveries. I guess he went to the funeral home on his lunchbreak, but he's back to work now." He looks over his shoulder at Laurent seated in the interrogation room. "Depending on how this goes, I may not need to talk to Erik Sinclair after all."

I'm not sure if he's really that optimistic or if that statement was wishful thinking.

We follow him into the room.

"Now, should I call Ivy to come down here as well?" Detective Bilson asks Laurent.

"No. Leave her out of this. I'll tell you what you want to know."

"Really? You're not asking for your lawyer?"

Riley and I exchange puzzled looks. Why would Laurent lawyer up yesterday and then decide to talk without his lawyer today?

"I'll tell you what I know."

More like what he wants us to know. I'm getting the feeling he wants it to appear as though he's being cooperative. He probably thinks that will help him since he was caught tampering with the crime scene.

"I'm listening," Detective Bilson says, taking a seat across from Laurent and getting out his notepad and pen to write things down.

"I thought you were going to ask me questions," Laurent says.

"I have a question." I raise my hand like I'm in school, and instantly, I lower it, feeling foolish for the action.

"Go ahead, Hailey," Detective Bilson says.

"Why are you keeping Vance from his wife's will?"

"I'm not. The flash drive you heard us talking about didn't contain a will. It contained a business plan. One where Simone planned to cut me out of the business entirely."

"Then how did you know she planned to leave all her money to her own company?" I ask.

"It was mentioned in the business plan, but I haven't seen the will."

"What flash drive did Ivy give to Vance?" I sit down next to Detective Bilson.

"She found two in Simone's belongings at the house. The first one was labeled 'will.' That's the one she gave to Vance."

"Why did she decide to keep the second?" Detective Bilson asks.

"Because Ivy knew Simone was up to something. Simone was having all these secret meetings."

"With whom?" I ask.

"Some were with Ruby Redford. Others were with lawyers or accountants. I had a feeling she was planning to cut me out of the business."

"Don't you mean she was planning to leave the boutique and branch out on her own?" That makes more sense to me.

"It's the same thing. We were business partners. Leaving is no different than cutting me out."

"But it wasn't like she was trying to take the boutique from you," Detective Bilson says. "I get what Hailey's saying."

"I'm a numbers person. That's why Simone partnered with me. I don't know a thing about fashion. What am I going to do with a boutique without a fashion expert like Simone to run it?"

"But you already have contracts with the designers Simone brought in. You were looking over their contracts in your office."

"I knew you were in my office," he says.

Oops. I didn't mean to out myself, but I suppose it's best to get everything in the open now. "Yes, and I saw the contracts on your desk."

"I was trying to find out if the designers were obligated to work with Belle Boutique for a specified amount of time or if they could simply walk away with Simone when she left."

"And?" Detective Bilson asks.

Laurent looks down at the table.

"You know I can get a warrant to obtain those contracts. You're already in big trouble for tampering with my crime scene," Detective Bilson says.

"The contracts state that the designers are tied to Simone. Meaning, if she left, they'd go with her."

"Which also means, killing Simone freed those designers to stay with you," I say.

Laurent Vincent lowers his head and cries. "I know how this looks, but I didn't kill my sister."

"When did you discover this link between the designers and your sister, Mr. Vincent?" Detective Bilson asks.

Laurent raises his head. "I'd like my lawyer now."

CHAPTER FOURTEEN

Ben drives me back to Riley's townhouse since that's where my car is parked. We all have dinner together because we're starving after following Simone's family around all day and not stopping to eat anything.

Marley jumps up onto the couch and settles on my lap.

"Well, I guess you aren't leaving any time soon," Riley says. "You've been claimed."

Marley starts purring loudly as if to confirm it.

"Luckily, I'm both full and comfortable."

We ate the biggest cheesesteaks I've ever seen along with onion rings, loaded potato skins, and fries. I'm not sure I could get up off this couch if I wanted to after all that food. But considering we were eating two meals at once, I guess it was appropriate.

"Do you think Detective Bilson will release Maxwell Decker after what Laurent said in that interrogation room today?" Ben reaches over to scratch the top of Marley's head. Marley leans into it for a few seconds before standing up and climbing onto Ben's lap.

"I guess Marley traded up," I say with a laugh.

"Nah. He'll realize he downgraded," Ben says.

Marley climbs onto Ben's shoulder and nuzzles his neck.

"No, I think he really likes you."

"Back to your question," Riley interrupts. "No, I don't think Garrett will release Maxwell yet. Laurent's lawyer wouldn't let him answer any more of Garrett's questions, so there isn't much of a case to be made against him just yet."

"Garrett found definite motive and caught Laurent tampering with the crime scene. I'd say he looks as guilty as Maxwell when he was found with the murder weapon." I shrug.

"I don't know. Does tampering with evidence trump holding the murder weapon?" Riley asks.

"Don't forget the killer always returns to the scene of the crime." So far, I've actually found that to be very true. I never would have thought it would be, but on each case I've helped investigate, it's happened.

"Laurent couldn't exactly leave the crime scene though since he works there," Riley says.

"Are you trying to prove his innocence?" I ask.

"Not at all. I totally think he did it. I just like playing devil's advocate." She smirks.

"It's good to see you don't only do that sort of thing when Detective Bilson is around," Ben says.

"Nah. I'll give anyone a hard time," she jokes, though part of me thinks that's actually true.

"Do you think Ivy knows?" I ask. "I mean it's possible Laurent discovered Simone was up to something and killed her without telling anyone. Ivy might think she's helping her husband save his business after someone murdered her sister-in-law. She might not have any clue that Laurent is the killer."

Riley's brow creases in thought. "I suppose. She wanted the will, but that might have been to try to save the business."

"But remember how Ivy and Laurent took separate cars to the funeral service," Ben says. "What if Ivy suspects Laurent after Detective Bilson questioned them both together the other day?"

Riley wags a finger at him. "That makes sense. I wonder if she went to the station to be with Laurent after the lawyer was called."

"Why don't you ask Detective Bilson?" I say.

"Why don't you? You two text now." There's a hint of jealousy in her tone, which is absurd since she knows I'm interested in Ben, not Garrett Bilson.

"We only text to discuss the case."

"This is about the case," Riley counters.

"I know, but you two are…friends."

"Hardly."

"Okay, but you've known him a lot longer."

"I'm not a secretary, Hailey. If you want to text Garrett, text him." Riley's voice gets louder with each word.

Ben stiffens beside me. "I hate to do this to you, Marley, but I'm going to head out."

"Ben, you don't have to leave," Riley says. "I'm sorry I yelled." She looks at me. "Really, I'm sorry. I don't know why I'm so worked up right now."

Repressing your feelings will do that to a person, but I don't say that out loud.

"It's okay."

"No, it's not. You didn't do anything to deserve that. Maybe I should go to bed."

We all stand up, and Ben puts Marley down on the couch. "See you next time, little guy."

"Get some rest," I tell Riley.

"Hails, I really am sorry."

"I forgive you," I tell her, giving her a hug.

Ben walks me to my car. "Any plans for tomorrow?"

"Not yet. I'm hoping Detective Bilson will keep us updated on what's going on with Laurent."

"Can I pick you up for breakfast then?"

"I'd like that."

He opens my car door for me, and I get inside, lowering the window as soon as I start the engine. Ben leans down, placing his arms on the open window. "Sleep well, Hailey."

"You too."

"This is the part where you kiss her goodnight," Riley says from her front door. "How do you two manage when I'm not around?"

"Good night, Riley," I call to her.

She shakes her head and goes inside.

"I wasn't sure if we were to the point where we kiss goodbye," Ben says.

"Don't listen to Riley. I think all single people love to give relationship advice and fail to see the irony in the fact that they aren't in a relationship themselves."

"You know I think you're right about that." He laughs, but then he leans forward to kiss me goodnight. "See you in the morning."

"See you," I say.

I'm pulling into my driveway when I realize I'm still smiling. My time in Rockland has been…well, rocky, but Ben has been a bright spot amidst the murder investigations and awful jobs I've had. I'm really glad I met him.

George, the British waiter at the diner, tops off my coffee for me as I take my last bite of French toast. "How was everything?"

"Delicious." I lower my voice. "I think it was the extra powdered sugar you put on top for me."

George raises one finger to his lips. "Shh." He winks at me before pulling our check out of his apron pocket and placing it on the table for us. "No rush. Take your time."

"Thanks, George," Ben says, reaching for the bill.

"You have to let me pay this time." I hold my hand out for the check.

"I invited you. You're absolutely not paying."

Ben knows about my money troubles, but I've been working since I moved here. I'm not totally broke. Sure, I never have food in my refrigerator, but that's because I'm trying to save every penny I have. Between rent and utilities, it eats up most of my paycheck. But Jane Honda isn't getting any younger, and one of these days I really am going to have car trouble that costs me and arm and a leg to have repaired. I have to have money in the bank just in case.

"Next time it's my treat," I say.

"We'll see." Ben pulls some bills out of his wallet and places them on the table with the check. "Any word from Detective Bilson?"

"No," I say before sipping my coffee.

"How about Riley?"

"Nope. I think she probably slept in this morning. Marley's most likely curled up on top of her head, shielding the sunlight from her view."

"He sleeps on her head?"

"Every night, according to Riley."

Ben laughs. "He's an interesting cat."

"To say the least."

After we both finish our coffee, we head back out to Ben's truck. "You want to go to the station to check in with Detective Bilson?"

Instead of answering, I stare in the direction of Belle Boutique.

"Hailey?" Ben asks. He stands next to me and follows my gaze. "Who opened the boutique this morning?"

"That's what I'm wondering."

Ben takes my hand, lacing his fingers through mine. For a moment, I'm so surprised by the gesture I don't move, and I'm jerked forward slightly when he starts walking across the street. "Are you okay?" He looks down at our hands. "Is this not all right?"

I smile at him. "It's more than all right," I say, catching up.

As we approach the boutique, I see Jesse inside. "Jesse?"

Ben opens the door for me, and I step inside first.

"Oh, hi, Hailey," Jesse says. "Are you working today, too?"

"When did you get back in town?" I ask, completely ignoring his question.

"Yesterday. I called Laurent and apologized for taking off without telling him. When I explained what happened with my mom, he said he completely understood. I asked if I still had a job, and he asked me to come in to work today." Jesse raises his arms at his sides and lowers them again. "So, here I am."

That must have happened before Laurent was taken into police custody. I doubt Jesse has any idea that's where our boss is right now. "Are things okay with your mom?"

"Not exactly. I haven't told her I'm back. I'm eighteen, so I can legally live on my own. I'm renting a studio apartment with my own money, so I can do whatever I want, and she doesn't have a say at all anymore. My roof, my rules." He leans toward me. "That's what she always told me, and I hated it. But now I can use those words against her." He smiles, looking rather pleased with himself.

"Well, it's good to have you back." This might be the perfect opportunity to check out Laurent's office again since Jesse has no idea what's been going on around here. "I have to go get something," I tell him. "I'll be right back. Ben, would you come with me?"

"Of course," Ben says.

We walk down the hallway to Laurent's office. I try the door-knob, but it's locked. "Darn it. I was hoping to get a look at those contracts with the designers."

"Why? Laurent already confessed to the contents. I don't think any of it was a lie since it was pretty incriminating. No one would try to get themselves arrested."

"Let's try Simone's office," I say. "Maybe there's something in there that will give us a clue."

"Are you saying you're not convinced Laurent is the killer?'

"I'm saying I don't think we have enough evidence against him yet. Detective Bilson will need more if he wants to build a strong case for conviction."

"I'm surprised Simone's office isn't blocked off."

"I guess since Jesse and Ruby were in Simone's office when she was killed it made it a room of little interest to the police."

I open the door and step inside. The office looks nothing like Laurent's. Instead of a desk, there are several chairs and a settee arranged in an oval. A coffee table is positioned in the middle. Around the walls are dummies displaying dresses and other cloth-ing.

"She really was the artistic sibling," Ben says.

"From what I overheard, Simone was selling some of her own designs under Ruby Redford's name."

"Think she was too afraid to put her own name on her designs before she figured out if the public would like them?"

"Maybe. I don't suppose it's easy to put your work out there for other people to judge. Taste is subjective and differs from one person to the next. I'm sure these designers take a lot of criticism."

"I don't doubt they do."

I don't see anything in here that gives me a clue as to why anyone would kill Simone.

"Hailey?" Jesse calls before walking into the office. "What are you doing?"

"I thought I left something in here the other day."

"What was it? Maybe I've seen it around."

"A flash drive." It's the first thing that pops into my head.

Jesse furrows his brow. "I haven't seen one, but I'll keep a lookout for it."

"Thanks. So, how much do you remember from the evening Simone died?" My segue is terrible, but Jesse doesn't seem to notice.

"Um, just that Ruby and I were talking about some of my designs when I heard you scream."

"Did you see Simone before you went into her office?" I ask.

"No. Her office was empty. I was going to bring Ruby in and have her wait while I found Simone, but like I said, we were discussing one of my designs, and I guess I got a little carried away."

"How long would you say you were in the office?"

"I don't know. Not too long. I mean you and Leslie saw us go back here, right?"

We did. It didn't seem long at all. "Yeah." I guess I have to tell him the latest theory. "The police are looking into Laurent as a possible suspect."

"Laurent? Why? I thought they caught the killer already. It was the delivery guy."

"Turns out it wasn't him. He just found the body and tried to get the clothes rack off Simone to help her."

"He really didn't do it?"

I shake my head. "I don't think so."

"But why would Laurent kill his own sister?"

"Apparently, Simone had planned to leave the boutique and Laurent behind to start her own design company. Laurent and his wife believe Ruby Redford was helping her."

Jesse's jaw drops open. "I wonder if that's what she meant."

"Meant by what?"

"Ruby said she had a feeling I'd be able to show my work soon."

Simone was planning to showcase her own work, not other people's. But then again, Laurent believed she planned to take the designers with her, so maybe her company would showcase her own work as well as the work of the designers she was working with.

"Everyone thought Simone was the mean sibling," Jesse says, "but Ruby really liked her. She said Simone was misunderstood, like a lot of creative types can be."

"Are you saying you think Laurent was the meaner sibling after all?"

"All I know is Laurent cares about numbers. If he was worried about losing his career…" Jesse sighs. "I'm going to have to find a new job, aren't I?"

I think we both are.

CHAPTER FIFTEEN

I convince Jesse that locking up for the day is the best course of action given that Laurent is in police custody. He goes back to his apartment, but not before asking Ben if his temp agency can find him a new job. Ben takes his number and promises to get back to him as soon as he has a lead.

We go to the police station to talk to Detective Bilson.

"Why does a high school student have keys to get into the boutique?" Detective Bilson asks after we tell him what happened.

"I don't know." I didn't even stop to consider that. "I knew Leslie had a key, but she's there most days and has been working at the boutique for years."

Yet Simone still didn't know her name. Something isn't adding up.

"Jesse made it sound like Simone wasn't as bad as most people thought, yet Simone called Leslie by the wrong name."

"What name did she use?" Detective Bilson asks.

"Charlene. Laurent told her Charlene quit four months ago." Is this a case of an awful person dying and then people misremembering how bad they really were because they feel sorry the person died so young? Could that be what's happening here?

"Maybe Simone had two sides to her," Ben suggests. "One for the people she liked, and one for the people she didn't care about."

"Maybe." I lean back in the chair across from Detective Bilson.

"Laurent's lawyer is sticking to the story that Laurent merely had a temporary lapse in judgement after grieving at the funeral and accidentally opened the back door out of habit," Detective Bilson says.

"Convenient story," I say.

"That's what I think. And he's claiming that's when Laurent noticed the chime wasn't working on the door, and he tried to fix it himself."

I guess money can buy lawyers who are capable of spinning any story in their client's favor.

Money. "Detective, Jesse mentioned Laurent was the numbers guy. That's the part of the business he controlled. So how was Simone able to plot to take half the business right out from under him?"

"I couldn't tell you. What I can tell you is that Laurent's lawyer is claiming emotional distress. He said nothing Laurent has admitted to is admissible because he's beside himself with grief and betrayal."

"Can he really do that?"

"He's bringing in a psychologist to analyze Laurent and support the claim," Detective Bilson says.

"And if this psychologist, who I'm sure is on Laurent's payroll, makes this claim, does that mean your case against him falls apart?"

"Well, I'm allowed to ask for a second psychological evaluation at that point."

"And if it differs from the original one?" I ask.

"Then a few different things have to happen, all of which will take time."

Meaning the case is stalled, which I'm sure is exactly what the lawyer wants to happen because it will get him the time he needs to disprove everything Detective Bilson has amassed against Laurent thus far.

"You need more evidence."

"I'm working on getting a warrant to search Laurent's office."

Good. "Have you spoken to Vance Brooks?"

"Briefly. He said he doesn't want to create a family dispute over a rumor of a secret will. He said he believes if Simon really had one she would have told him and left instructions."

"But I thought he did know there was a will."

"That was what he originally told us, but now he's saying that he believes Simone decided against one."

This family changes their stories to suit their own needs.

"I know what you're thinking, Hailey, but you should not go anywhere near Vance Brooks. I don't believe he killed his wife, so it's not worth it to anger a man like him by asking a bunch of questions that won't help solve this case." Detective Bilson locks eyes with me. "Am I making myself clear?"

"Crystal. Have you talked to Riley lately?"

"No, why?"

"I was just wondering." I remember the video I took of Laurent tampering with the door, the same video where Riley insulted Detective Bilson before I stopped recording. I have to give it to him if it will help him with his case against Laurent. "I almost forgot that I took a video of Laurent messing around with the back door of the boutique." I pull out my phone.

"You did?" Detective Bilson sounds really happy about that.

"Um, yeah, but before you watch it, you should know Riley's only joking at the end of it."

He leans back in his chair. "What did she do?"

"Remember how Laurent sort of opened the door into your face?"

Detective Bilson covers his face with his hand. "That's on your video?"

"Sorry but yes."

He sighs. "I still need it."

"I figured. Should I text it to you?"

"That will be fine. Thanks, Hailey."

I send the video and turn to Ben. "Can I have a word with Detective Bilson in private? It will only take a minute."

"Of course. I'll wait in the truck."

"Thank you." I smile at him as he walks out.

"What's up?" Detective Bilson asks.

"It's about Riley. She thinks you know her too well, and that scares her."

"Of course, I know her well. I've known her all her life."

"Exactly. She doesn't like feeling vulnerable. It makes her lash out so she appears tougher. You have to be able to read between the lines with her."

"What are you saying?" He cocks his head at me.

"I think you two are more alike than you realize."

"We're polar opposites." He lets out a huff.

"You're not. You're both stubborn when it comes to admitting how you feel. You both know things about the other that make you uncomfortable. And you both really care about each other but don't want to make that known."

"Did she tell you this?"

"You know Riley. She'd never say it out loud, but she also doesn't need to."

"I don't know what to do with this information."

"I don't either, but I thought you should know." I stand up. "Please don't ever tell her we had this conversation."

"Riley hates when people talk about her behind her back. I'd never say anything to her about this."

"Good luck with the case." I walk out of the station and to Ben's car.

"Everything okay?" he asks, starting the engine.

"Yeah, it's fine. Sorry about that, but I knew it was going to be an awkward conversation to begin with, and I thought it would be better if it was just him and me."

"Should I be worried?" He looks at me briefly before backing out of his parking spot.

"About what?" Realization dawns on me. "Oh! No. No, no, no. I wanted to talk to him about Riley. That's all it was about. He knows I like you." I don't mean for the last part to come out, but when I see the smile it brings to Ben's face, I'm glad it did.

"What would you like to do today since you don't have to work? We could go have a picnic in the park, see a movie, anything you'd like."

"How about go talk to a wealthy widower about his brother-in-law?"

"Please tell me that's a joke." He eyes me briefly.

"Laurent's lawyer is good. The only hope we have of getting evidence against him is to convince Vance Brooks that Laurent has the secret will and a fancy-talking lawyer who can bury Vance if he takes him to court over Simone's money."

"You really think that will work?"

"I need it to for Maxwell Decker's sake."

We drive to Vance Brooks's house. This time he's home when we knock. Thank goodness for Sundays.

His expression when he opens the door says enough, but he chooses to toss out a disgruntled, "What are you two doing here?" all the same.

"We need to talk to you about your brother-in-law," I say. "I'm sure you're aware he's currently in police custody."

"I'm sure he won't be there for long. He has good lawyers."

"Yes, he does. I've heard all about how they're trying to get the charges against Laurent dropped. But that's not a good thing for you, is it?"

"Why would that possibly be bad for me?" He leans on the doorframe.

"Well, if Laurent is in jail, he wouldn't be able to contest the will."

"My wife didn't leave a will."

"Oh, yes, she did. And Laurent doesn't want you to see it. But he and Ivy both have read it. I overheard them talking about it."

"Why should I believe you?" He crosses his arms as well as his legs. I'm not sure how he's not toppling over standing like that.

"What reason would I have for lying?" I ask. "Besides, I can tell you loved your wife. I think you deserve to know the truth and decide for yourself what to do with it. The flash drive with the will is in Laurent's office at the boutique."

"I have the flash drive Ivy found. There's no will on it, though it is labeled as such."

So he thinks Simone had a change of heart and didn't write one.

"Ivy found two flash drives that day. The other one details how she was leaving her money to her own clothing line. She was taking her part of the business from Laurent. The designers were contracted to go where Simone went."

"You think my wife was cutting her brother out of the business?"

"Yes, and I think he discovered her plan and killed her to stop her."

"But you said these plans were on the flash drive Ivy found after Simone died." Vance stands up straight. I have his full attention now.

"That's right. I think Laurent suspected Simone was up to something and killed her. Then he discovered her full plan after the fact."

"Why are you telling me this?"

"So you can use this information to make sure Laurent doesn't get away with murdering your wife."

"How do you expect me to do that?"

"You can press charges against Ivy for theft."

"Theft?" He jerks his head back.

"She stole from Simone's room. She took both flash drives. With Simone dead, they belong to you."

"What will charging Ivy with theft do, though?"

It will tie up Laurent's lawyer and give Detective Bilson more time to build his case. "Mr. Brooks, I'm not going to tell you what to do, but if my brother-in-law and sister-in-law were trying to steal from me, I'd do something about it. If you get them on this theft, you'll have more ground to stand on if they try to take Simone's half of the business from you. You can stop them and maybe even help the police catch Simone's killer." I look him directly in the eye. "Call Detective Bilson. He'll help you."

"You were there when Simone died," Vance says.

I nod. "I was. I found the deliveryman with her."

"But you don't think he killed her."

"He had no reason to."

"Most people hated my wife." His tone softens. "That's why we had such a small service. I couldn't bear the thought of opening it to the public and having no one show up. So I only invited family."

"And Ruby Redford," I say.

"Ruby is family. Simone took care of her. She made her into a star. Ruby appreciated everything Simone did for her." He wipes a tear from his eye. "Everyone needs a friend in this world. My wife only had two. Me and Ruby, but we were enough for her."

"What about Laurent?" Ben asks. "Did he and Simone not get along?"

"They did at first, but as the years passed, they fought more and more. Simone followed her gut, and she was a visionary. Laurent followed the numbers. I can see why she didn't want to keep working with him. I just wish she would have told me. I would have supported her one hundred percent."

"Call Detective Bilson," I say again.

He nods and closes the door.

"Do you think he'll actually do it?" Ben asks as we get back into his truck.

"I hope so."

Since we haven't seen Riley yet today, we drive to her townhouse. To my surprise, a patrol car is parked outside. Ben and I exchange a look as we walk up to Riley's front door. I debate turning around and leaving in case Detective Bilson is here, and they're actually talking things through. But then I hear Riley yell.

I open the door, and a football comes speeding right at my head. Ben catches it before it hits me.

Riley laughs. "Sorry, Hailey!"

"What's going on?" I ask, out of breath from fear.

"Um, I stopped by to talk to Riley, and we…" Detective Bilson turns to Riley for help.

"Okay, so we were in gym class together one year, and we were supposed to learn how to throw a spiral."

"Only Riley can't throw if her life depended on it," Detective Bilson says.

"I can throw. I just can't throw a spiral," she corrects him.

"Okay, fair enough." He holds up his hands in surrender.

"So anyway, Garrett gets the brilliant idea to make me mad."

"Because she was overthinking it. I figured if I made her angry, she wouldn't put too much thought into the throw, and it would go better."

"How's that for some sound logic?" Riley rolls her eyes, but I actually see Detective Bilson's point.

"I guess it didn't go well?" I ask.

"No, it worked!" Detective Bilson says. "She threw a perfect spiral, but it hit our gym teacher square in the eye. He had to wear an eye patch for the rest of the semester."

Riley laughs. "Every time he'd tell us what to do in class, we'd salute him and say, "Aye, aye, matey!"" She doubles over in laughter.

"So what just happened here?" Ben asks, tossing the football back to Detective Bilson.

"I asked Riley if she still had that arm, and she whipped out a football. I was so surprised she even owned one."

"What do you mean? That's the same one I hit Mr. Feeney with. I kept it."

"You stole it from gym class?"

Riley puts her hands on her hips in challenge. "What are you going to do? Arrest me for it all these years later?"

I'm pretty sure neither one of them has a clue they're flirting with each other right now.

Detective Bilson's phone rings. "It's Vance Brooks," he says, after reading the screen. His gaze lifts to meet mine. "Hailey, did you go see him?"

I bob one shoulder. "Maybe."

He groans and puts the football on the couch before answering the call. "Detective Bilson. Yes, Mr. Brooks. Absolutely. Can you meet me at the station? I can be there in about five minutes. Great. Thank you." He pockets his phone. "He said you visited him with an interesting story today."

"I thought it might help your case against Laurent," I say.

"You really need to stay out of this, Hailey."

"I think you mean 'thank you, Hailey,'" Riley says.

"No, I meant what I said. I asked her to stay away from Vance Brooks, and she did the exact opposite. I don't mind sharing information with you, but if you're going to blatantly disregard my warnings, I won't be able to anymore."

"She did you a favor," Riley says, standing up and getting in Detective Bilson's face.

Great. They were getting along so well, and I came in and ruined everything. "I'm sorry. You're right. I shouldn't have gotten involved when you asked me not to. It won't happen again."

"Don't apologize to him." Riley whips around to face me and throws her arm out in Detective Bilson's direction, hitting him square in the stomach. "He should be apologizing to you."

"I have to go," Detective Bilson says, walking past Riley and right out the door.

Riley slumps down on the couch. "He's such a jerk."

"No, he's not," I say, sitting next to her.

"Yes, he is. Even Marley knows it. He won't come downstairs when Garrett is here."

Most likely because Riley is usually yelling at Detective Bilson. Animals are great at sensing human emotions.

Riley's phone rings, but she doesn't answer it.

"Don't you want to see who it is?"

"It's Garrett. I don't want to talk to him."

He tries again, but she ignores that call, too. On the third attempt, I grab her phone and pick it up. "Hello?" I answer.

"Hailey?" His voice is faint.

"Are you okay?" I ask.

"I was in an accide…"

"Detective? Are you there?"

CHAPTER SIXTEEN

Riley grabs the phone from my hand. "Quit messing around, Garrett. You're freaking out Hailey." She pauses. "Garrett?"

"He said he was in an accident," I tell her.

"We need to go find him," Ben says. "Come on."

We run outside to Ben's truck, and he peels out. We don't have to go far to find the accident. The road is a mess. Cars are at a standstill. I get on my phone and call 911 even though I'm sure several other onlookers have done so already. The operator informs me the police and ambulances are already en route.

Riley gets out of the truck.

"Go with her," Ben tells me. "I'll stay with the truck."

I get out and hurry after her. When we get closer, we see the patrol car wrapped around a lamppost. I'm not sure how anyone could have survived a crash like that.

Riley screams and runs toward the car.

I'm well aware there's a big risk of the car catching fire and even exploding, but I can't stop myself from following Riley.

She tries to open the driver's side door, but it's stuck. She bangs on the window. "Garrett! Garrett! Look at me!"

He doesn't move inside the car.

A few other people get out of their cars and come to help us.

"The door won't open," I tell a man holding a crow bar.

"Stand back," he tells us. He uses the crow bar to smash the window.

Pete Modell runs over to us. "Is that Garrett Bilson inside that car?" he asks us.

Riley is sobbing now, but she manages to bob her head.

Pete pushes the man with the crow bar aside. "We have to pull him out through the window. That door isn't going to budge."

The sirens in the background are getting closer.

Pete leans through the window, unclicks the seat belt, and lifts Detective Bilson out of the vehicle through the window. As soon as Detective Bilson is partially through the window, I grab his legs to help Pete get him out.

"Riley, Hailey, get away from the car. I don't want you anywhere near it if it catches fire," Pete says. He puts Detective Bilson over his shoulder. "Go! Both of you. Run!"

I grab Riley's arm and pull her away. Pete follows us as quickly as he can. We don't get that far before the car goes up in flames. People all around us scream. Pete brings Detective Bilson to a grassy area and lays him down.

"Is he alive?" Riley asks.

Pete leans down. "He's breathing, but it's faint."

The paramedics arrive on the scene and immediately rush over to us. "Is that Detective Bilson?" the female EMT asks us.

"Yes," Pete says. "He needs immediate medical attention. I have no idea the extent of his injuries, and I had to rip him out of that car."

The woman looks at the car. "You did the right thing. We'll take it from here."

"I want to go with him," Riley says.

"Only a family member or spouse can go with him. I'm sorry," she says.

"We'll go to the hospital," I tell her. "Ben will take us."

"He's stuck in that traffic."

"Then we'll take a taxi," I say. "I will get you to the hospital one way or another."

It's late when we finally get word from the doctor that Detective Bilson is stable. He suffered a concussion, lacerations to the face, arms, and chest, and a few broken ribs. According to the doctor, it could have been a lot worse, but police officers undergo training for surviving crashes resulting from high speed chases.

"How did this happen?" Riley asks after the doctor leaves us. "He was on his way to the station to meet with Vance Brooks. "He shouldn't have been speeding."

I know how it happened, but she won't want to hear it. Detective Bilson was upset with her. He probably wasn't paying attention and crashed.

"They aren't going to let us in to see him either because we aren't family."

"Does he have family in town?" I ask.

"Not anymore. I can call his parents, though." She pulls out her phone.

"You should. Someone needs to tell them." I stand up. "I'll go look for some bad vending machine coffee in the meantime."

"Thanks."

I walk down the hallway and run into Ben. As soon as I see him, I throw my arms around him. "I'm so glad you're here."

"The road was closed for hours while they cleaned up after the accident. I wish I could have been here sooner."

That's what happens when you live in a tiny town without the resources to handle emergencies like this. Everything takes that much longer.

"The doctor said he's stable. His injuries were much more minor than they anticipated. He's still unconscious, though. I think the concussion is the worst of it. Though the broken ribs will hurt like crazy when he wakes up."

"Promise me something," Ben says, taking my hand in his.

"What?" I ask.

"If you're ever mad at me, don't get behind the wheel. I don't care if you have to scream at me or punch me until you feel better, but don't ever drive angry like that. Promise me."

"I'd never punch you," I say. Truthfully, I can't even imagine being angry with him. Ben is like the sweetest man alive.

"Detective Bilson should have known better," Ben says.

Yes, he should have, but Riley has always gotten to him like that. "Those two might be the death of each other if they don't admit their feelings soon."

"Let's hope this is the thing that finally knocks some sense into both of them." Ben wraps an arm around my shoulders, and we search for some coffee. We finally find a vending machine at the end of a hallway.

"Hey," a nurse calls in a hushed voice. "You don't want to drink that stuff."

"Is there anything better?" I ask.

"How many do you need?" she asks me.

"Three." I hold up three fingers.

"Wait there." She disappears back inside the doorway she was peeking out of. When she returns two minutes later, she's balancing three cups in her hands. "This is from the nurses' station. It's much better than that junk they put in the vending machine."

"Thank you," I say, taking a coffee from her. Ben grabs the other two.

"I heard about some people pulling Detective Bilson from his car before it caught fire. I'm guessing that was you guys."

"Well, Pete Modell actually pulled him from the car, but my friend Riley and I were there to help. Ben got stuck in all that traffic and missed most of the nightmare."

The nurse looks at Ben. "You're the lucky one then." She turns back to me. "Sometimes people have nightmares after witnessing something like that, so if you do, feel free to come back here and talk to me. It helps when you talk about it."

"Thank you. You're really very sweet."

"I'm nurse Maggie."

"I'm Hailey, and this is Ben."

"Nice to meet you both. I should get back to work, but if there's anything I can do for you, just let me know."

"Actually, is there any way you can get my friend Riley in to see Detective Bilson?" I ask.

"Is she his girlfriend?"

"They have a complicated relationship."

"Ah. I see. Tell you what. Let me do the rounds and make sure no one is scheduled to check on Detective Bilson in the next twenty minutes. Then I'll come get your friend. Where is she?"

"In the waiting area by room 312. That's where Detective Bilson is."

"Great. That will make it easier to find you." She squeezes my arm before starting her rounds.

Ben and I return to Riley and tell her about Nurse Maggie.

Riley drinks all her coffee in about two long gulps. "I needed that. Thank you. I'm surprised vending machine coffee is so tolerable."

"That's because it's not. Nurse Maggie hooked us up with the good stuff. She heard about how some civilians saved Detective Bilson. I think this was her version of rewarding us for a good deed."

"And she can really get me inside his room?" Riley asks.

"That's what she said."

Riley taps her foot on the floor. She's not the most patient person.

Nurse Maggie comes by about four minutes later and waves Riley over to her. She sneaks Riley inside and mans the door. I doubt Riley will have much time inside the room, but hopefully seeing that Detective Bilson is okay will be enough to get her to calm down.

"Are you okay?" Ben asks me.

"Yeah. I'll be fine."

Nurse Maggie waves us over to her. "Did you two hear?"

"Hear what?" I'm afraid Detective Bilson took a turn for the worse, or the doctors discovered another injury that could be life-threatening.

"Turns out Detective Bilson swerved to miss hitting someone who ran out into the road."

"Who was it?" I ask.

"I'm not sure. But apparently this person didn't get away completely unscathed. We've gotten reports that someone was seen hobbling away from the scene of the crash."

"So they were injured?"

"It seems that way. We were told to be on the lookout for someone arriving with injuries that could have been caused by getting hit by a car."

Detective Bilson somehow hit this person, but not directly. He took the brunt of the crash himself by turning into the lamppost.

"I guess that means the police are looking for this person to figure out what happened," Ben says.

"Yes. Very few people saw the accident occur, and they were all observing from different angles. It's caused major differences in their accounts. Some reported saying it was a woman who ran out in front of the patrol car. Others said it was a man. One woman even swore she thought it was a child or teenager at the oldest." Nurse Maggie shakes her head. "If we don't find this person, we may not know for sure what happened."

"What about when Detective Bilson regains consciousness?" I ask.

"There's a very good chance he's going to suffer from amnesia. How much of his memory is affected is still unknown right now. We have to wait until he wakes up to find out for certain."

"You mean he might not remember the accident at all? Like short-term amnesia?" I ask.

"Yes, or it could be a lot worse. Most of his injuries were to his upper body. His head took the brunt of it. He may wake up and not even know who he is."

How am I going to tell Riley that?

Nurse Maggie opens the door to tell Riley it's time for her to go. I peek in on Detective Bilson. He's all wrapped up in white bandages. Most of his face is covered. If I didn't know it was him, I wouldn't recognize him at all.

I wrap my arm around Riley as she steps out of the room.

"Thank you," she tells Nurse Maggie.

"We'll take good care of him," Nurse Maggie assures her.

We leave the hospital and drive Riley home.

"Hailey, would you mind staying here tonight?" Riley asks as we pull up to her townhouse. "I'd rather not be alone."

"Of course." I unclick my seat belt.

"I can pick you up in the morning," Ben says, "and bring you home."

"Thank you." Without thinking, I lean over to kiss him good-bye. It feels like the natural thing to do, and it brings a smile to his face. "Good night."

"Sweet dreams, Hailey," Ben says.

Riley and I go inside her townhouse, and I give Ben a small wave.

"You do know we have to solve this case for him now," Riley says once we're inside getting Marley his dinner.

I know she's talking about Detective Bilson. "I think we've pretty much solved it."

"We need evidence, and since Vance Brooks never got to meet with Garrett today, we need to make sure he finds out everything we know and talks to another officer at the Rockland PD."

"He's going to be okay, Riley. You know that, right?" She knows I'm talking about Detective Bilson.

"I just don't want him to wake up and worry about this case."

That might not be an issue if he doesn't remember the murder at all. "Riles, sit down." I motion to the chair she's standing beside at the kitchen table.

"Why do you have that look on your face? You're scaring me." She pulls out the chair and practically slides down into it.

"Nurse Maggie said there might be some memory loss associated with Detective Bilson's concussion."

"Memory loss? Are you saying he might not remember the accident?"

"Or the case. Or maybe even who he is."

She looks like she's going to be sick.

I bend down next to her and hug her. "They won't know until he wakes up, but Nurse Maggie said it should only be temporary."

"How can they possibly know that if they don't know the full extent of his injuries yet?"

I can't answer that for her.

"I can't believe this."

"I think you should go to the hospital tomorrow and stay with him as much as they'll allow you to. You know they say people who are unconscious can still hear things being said."

"I thought that was people in comas," she says.

"Maybe. It can't hurt though, right?"

She looks at me. "I know I said I hated that he knew everything about me, but having him forget me completely would be so much worse."

"I know. Let's not jump to any conclusions just yet. He might wake up and be fine."

"If he is, he'll probably wake up, see me, and start yelling about how the accident was my fault."

"About that. Nurse Maggie said the police were getting conflicting reports about the accident, but witnesses reported that someone ran out in front of Garrett's car."

"You called him Garrett," she says. "You must be really worried about him to not call him Detective Bilson."

"He's important to you, so that makes him important to me." I hitch one shoulder.

"Who would run out in front of a car?" she asks, clearly avoiding my comment.

"I don't know. Some people thought it was a man. Others said it was a woman. but one person thought it was a teenager."

"We should have traffic cameras in town."

"You should get some rest," I tell her. "You look exhausted."

"Thanks. Kick me while I'm down, why don't you?"

"I didn't mean you look terrible, just that you look tired."

"Is there a difference?"

Marley nuzzles my leg now that he's finished eating his dinner. I bend down, scoop him up, and hand him to Riley. "Take him up to bed."

She cuddles him to her chest and stands up. "If you get a call from that nurse, wake me up immediately."

"I will." I don't tell her that I didn't give Nurse Maggie my number, and there's no way I'd be listed as Garrett Bilson's emergency contact. Truth be told, I wouldn't be shocked if Riley was.

I make my way into the living room and grab the throw blanket off the back of the couch. I lie down and stare at the ceiling. Tomorrow, I have to find evidence that Laurent Vincent murdered his sister to save his business. And I have to do it without any resources at the Rockland PD. I'm not sure how I can pull that off, but I can't let Riley and Garrett down.

CHAPTER SEVENTEEN

After we drop Riley off at the hospital to sit with Garrett as he recovers, Ben and I drive to Vance Brooks's house. He's locking his front door when we pull up. Ben and I rush out of the truck to stop Vance from getting into his car.

"Mr. Brooks, please wait," I say, running over to him.

He looks confused. "What are you two doing here?"

"We need to speak with you," I say. "Did you hear about Detective Bilson's accident yesterday?"

"Yes, I waited in the police station for hours." He sounds like it was a major inconvenience to him that a man almost died.

"So you didn't speak to any other officers at the station?" Ben asks.

"No. I need to talk to the detective handling my wife's investigation. Why would I talk to someone else?" His tone implies any idiot would understand that.

"Well, Detective Bilson is going to be in the hospital for a while. Someone else at the Rockland PD will need to take over the case for him."

"Just great."

Wow. I'd thought he was the most likeable of the family members since it seemed like he really did love his wife, but his complete lack of compassion for Detective Bilson is grating on my nerves right now.

"I don't understand how a man who is grieving the loss of his wife can't be even the slightest bit compassionate for the man who is trying to solve her murder. Detective Bilson almost died yesterday trying to find answers for you."

"Hailey." Ben pulls me back, and I realize I've advanced on Vance Brooks. "Easy."

I take a deep breath. "I'm starting to think you don't really want to find out what happened to your wife. I think you're okay with people believing her death was a random act of violence committed by a deliveryman." That's when it clicks. "You spoke to Laurent when you were at the station yesterday. That's why you've had a change of heart, isn't it?"

Vance Brooks's jaw tenses. "I don't have to speak to either of you. Now get out of my way and get off my property before I call the police and have you arrested for trespassing."

"Hailey, let's go." Ben pulls me back toward the truck.

"I'm not letting this go, Mr. Brooks. I'm going to find out what really happened."

Ben opens the passenger door for me. "It's probably not a good idea to anger a man that wealthy."

I know he's right, but I can only imagine how Laurent manipulated Vance yesterday. Once Ben is in the truck and backing out of the driveway, I say, "How can Vance be okay with Laurent killing his wife?"

"We don't know for sure that he did."

Is it possible I'm wrong about Laurent? If he really didn't know about Simone's plans until after she was killed, then there would be no motive.

"Only one person seemed to be privy to Simone's plans for her business."

"You mean Ruby Redford," Ben says.

I nod. "I think we need to talk to her. If she told Laurent about it, then that would prove he did know and had motive to kill Simone before she could put her plan into motion."

Ben bobs his head. "You're right. But do you think Ruby would tell us?"

"If she and Simone were as close as it seems they were, I don't think she'd try to help Laurent. It's more likely either something slipped out in conversation, or Simone told Laurent in the midst of a fight. We need to find out what Ruby knows and how it might implicate Laurent."

Whenever I need to find someone in town, I go to Riley. She's like a living, breathing directory of Rockland, but she's busy with Garrett at the hospital, and I don't want to interrupt her in case he woke up.

"You don't know where Ruby lives, do you?" I ask Ben.

"No, and it's not like we can look her up because that's not even her real name."

"Her name is Rebecca. Leslie told me."

"Okay, that we can work with as long as Redford is her last name."

"It is."

Ben pulls over and starts searching on his phone. "This is interesting."

"What is?" I ask, leaning over the middle console to try to read his phone screen.

"When I look her up, it says Rebecca Redford is a designer living in New York City."

"Is it a different designer?" I ask.

"No, it's definitely her. There's a picture, and it mentions her design lines, Ruby and Red."

"Maybe Simone and Ruby planned to leave Rockland and pursue their new business venture in New York."

Ben turns to me. "That would mean Simone was planning to leave her husband as well."

My eyes widen. "If evidence of that was in the business plan on that flash drive, and Laurent told Vance about it at the station yesterday, that would explain why Vance no longer cares about solving his wife's murder."

"Because he learned that she was going to divorce him. How do we find Ruby?" Ben asks.

"Her address has to be on file at the boutique, but I don't have a key to get in."

"Doesn't Leslie?" Ben asks.

She does, but I can't ask her to break into the boutique with us. I don't want to get her in any trouble. I dial her number.

"Hailey?" she answers.

"Yes, it's me. Leslie, I need to ask you for something, but you can't ask any questions because I don't want you to get in any trouble or be able to answer those questions if the police talk to you later."

"Why would the police question me?" she asks, her voice shaky.

"They won't. I need you to leave the key to the boutique somewhere for me to find it."

"I don't understand."

"That's okay. Leave the key somewhere you could have dropped it. Like maybe on the sidewalk outside the boutique."

"What are you going to do?"

"I can't tell you."

"I don't know about this, Hailey."

"Are you planning to go back to work there?" I ask her.

"No. Definitely not. Not after what happened to Simone. And Laurent could be a murderer."

I get a better idea. "Okay, so what if you quit and hand the key to me because you don't want anything to do with the boutique or the Vincent family anymore?"

"Then I'd have to tell the police I gave you the key if they asked me."

"I know. I'll deal with that problem when I come to it. Right now, I just need that key."

"Is Laurent still being held by the police?"

I have no idea. Without Detective Bilson, I have no insight as to what's going on at the police station. "I'm not a hundred percent positive."

She doesn't say anything, which means she's still too nervous to agree to my plan.

"How about this? You write a letter to Laurent, telling him you're quitting. Put it in an envelope with the key. I'll take that from you, and you'll be off the hook."

"All right. I'll meet you outside the boutique in ten minutes." She hangs up.

Ben drives us to Town Square, and we park in front of the boutique. No lights are on, so that makes me think Laurent is still being held by the police. I thought with his fancy-talking lawyer, he might be out by now. If he is though, he isn't coming to work.

Leslie pulls up next to me and lowers her window. She's wearing big sunglasses and a hat, like she doesn't want to be recognized by anyone. She hands me an envelope through the window. And without so much as a word, she backs out of the parking spot and drives away.

"That was a little strange," Ben says.

"You're telling me." I open the envelope and pull out the key. As far as anyone else in town knows, I still work at the boutique. I never actually quit, so it's a technicality I can play off. It even makes sense that Leslie would turn in her resignation and key to me since I'm an employee, and Laurent is being detained. "Ready?" I ask Ben.

He nods, and we walk up to the boutique. I let us inside, but I don't turn on the lights. I'd rather people not know someone is here. We go directly to Laurent's office, but I stop short when I see the door is open. A woman is inside the office. I've only met her once, but I recognize her as Cynthia Lynch.

"Cynthia?" I say.

She jumps and whirls around. "You scared me half to death."

"Sorry. What are you doing here? And how did you get in?"

Her gaze goes to the storage room.

"You know the keycode?" I ask.

"All the designers do," she says.

"But that's an active crime scene," Ben says.

"I didn't touch anything or disrupt the crime scene in any way. I'm just looking for the check Laurent promised me. It should be here."

That's right. She came here the other day to complain about her check. She said she was being underpaid. "Did he straighten out the issue with your check?" I ask.

"Yes, or rather he said he did, but I can't seem to find the check." She rifles through the contracts on Laurent's desk. "He must have lied to me to get me to leave." She tosses a stack of papers back on the desk, and a few fall to the floor. "He's no better than his cheating, lying sister."

"What do you mean?" I ask.

"I'll show you." She storms out of the office and heads to a display of handbags. "See this." She holds up a bag, showing us the price tag. "This is what she charges, but she tells me she ran a sale and the customer didn't pay this price, so, therefore, my cut is much lower than the ticket price. But it's a lie. This *is* what she charges, and she pockets the difference!"

"Can you prove she was doing that?" I ask.

"If I could, do you think I'd be here right now looking for my money?"

"Then why do you keep selling your handbags here?" Ben asks. "Can you take them to another store?"

"No. My contract ties me to Simone."

"To Simone, but not the boutique, right?" I ask, confirming what I learned from the information on the flash drive and what Laurent told me.

"Yes."

"Did you know she was planning to leave Belle Boutique and start a new company?" I ask.

Cynthia narrows her eyes at me. "No. How do you know that's what she was going to do?"

"Laurent told me."

"What would have happened to you if she left?" Ben asks.

"I would have had to let her take my designs with her." She shakes her head. "Where was she going to go?"

"We think New York City. Apparently, Ruby Redford was the only one who knew about the plans before Simone died."

"Her precious Ruby." Cynthia scoffs. "I bet she never had to beg for money that was rightfully hers."

"Then you were aware of Ruby and Simone's friendship," I say.

"Everyone was aware of it."

I wonder if everyone was as bitter about it as Cynthia clearly is. Wait. She said the designers all have the keycode for the storage room. Any one of them could have used it on Monday to get inside the storage room and kill Simone. And if it was one of the designers, Simone wouldn't have feared them or suspected they'd try to harm her in any way. That's why she didn't scream or alert anyone she was in danger. She didn't know she was.

"Cynthia, are you and Ruby the only two designers Simone hired?"

"There was Erik Sinclair, but he was literally here for like a day before Simone canned him."

A day? "What happened?"

"He wanted too much money for his work. Simone fired him before they even signed the contract she had drawn up. I was here when the whole thing went down."

"When was that?"

"A week ago Sunday, I believe."

"You mean the day before Simone was murdered?"

"I guess so."

I look at Ben. "And Erik had the keycode for the back door?"

"Probably. All the employees get it."

Not the temps, apparently, because I was never given the code.

"I'm out of here," she says. "Tell Laurent I don't care if he's in jail. I want my check, or I will sue him for all the money I'm owed." She storms past us, but this time she uses the front door of the boutique.

Ben turns to me. "She seemed angry enough to murder someone."

"And she admitted to knowing the back keycode in addition to being enraged with Simone."

"Maybe Laurent didn't kill his sister after all," Ben says.

"Cynthia and Erik could be the more likely suspects. Either one could have snuck in the back door without anyone knowing." Laurent claims he was on the phone at the time of the murder. If his phone records prove that to be true, his lawyer will get the charges dropped in a heartbeat.

The front door to the boutique opens, and the lights come on. "It has to be Laurent," I whisper.

Ben pulls me into Simone's office, and we hide behind the door. Laurent walks past us, loosening his tie. He dials a number on the phone. "I'm at the office now. I should be home in about twenty minutes. MacMillan submitted my psych evaluation, which is putting everything on hold. I have to go to therapy now for a while, but it's worth it." He walks into his office, which makes it more difficult to hear what he's saying. "I don't have a clue who killed her, and I really don't care. She didn't get away with screwing me out of the business, and I don't have to deal with her anymore. It was exhausting having to play nice with everyone to make up for Simone's attitude. We're all better off without her." He pauses. "No, Vance won't be an issue. When he found out Simone contacted a divorce lawyer, he changed his tune rather quickly."

He must be talking to Ivy, filling her in on all she missed while he was in police custody. But why is he here? Is he getting the flash drive so he can destroy it before the police get the warrant to search his office?

"We can cash out the business and sell Simone's designs. I'll figure out the next step after that." He leaves the office, closing the door but not locking it, which means he took the flash drive. "I'm on my way."

Ben and I don't so much as breathe until Laurent leaves the boutique.

"Do you really believe he doesn't know who killed Simone?" Ben asks me. "Or do you think he just doesn't want Ivy to know he did it?"

"Ivy hated Simone. I don't think Laurent would have to hide it from his wife if he did kill his sister." And that means Laurent isn't the killer. That leaves one of the designers. But which one?

CHAPTER EIGHTEEN

Ben and I go to the diner to work through all this information over breakfast. I think better on a full stomach.

"Erik Sinclair had reason to hate Simone. They fought the day before she was killed, and she fired him, too." I'm thinking aloud as I eat.

"Did he seem like the violent type to you?"

"It's hard to say, but he definitely has anger issues."

"Yeah, we saw that at the funeral home. It's weird that he'd show up there if he killed Simone, though." Ben sips his coffee.

"Unless he thought it would make him look less guilty. And since the police had Maxwell Decker in custody for the murder, Erik didn't have much reason to be afraid he'd be caught."

"That's true."

"The other thing that's weird is all three designers showed their faces in the boutique on Monday before Simone was killed."

"That could be a coincidence, but I do see what you're saying. It's almost like the killer was trying to create an alibi, not for the actual murder, but more like a reason why they wouldn't have come to the boutique later since they'd already been there earlier in the day."

"All except Ruby, who was with Jesse when the murder happened," I say.

"Right. She's the only one with an actual alibi."

"Which means it has to be either Cynthia Lynch or Erik Sinclair." Both had motive. Both had means. Both had opportunity. "Think they were in on it together?"

"I guess that's possible. The two designers Simone screwed over ganging up to get revenge." Ben bobs his head before forking another bite of his omelet. "Have you heard from Riley at all today?"

I shake my head and take my phone out of my pocket. "I should text her and see if Garrett woke up yet."

"You're calling him Garrett now?" Ben asks.

"I get the feeling he'll be spending a lot more time with Riley in the near future, so I think it's only appropriate. Unless he's working, of course. Then I'll call him Detective Bilson."

Riley doesn't respond to my text right away, but reception in the hospital is spotty at best, and if she's in the room with Garrett, the nurses might have asked her to turn off her phone completely. I'm not sure what equipment in medical facilities can be affected by cell phones, but I've seen signs saying it's possible.

Ben is on his phone. "Erik Sinclair has Monday's off from work, right?"

"Yeah, that's why he was off last Monday when Simone was murdered."

"So he'd most likely be home today. I just found his address."

We finish eating, and even though I promised I'd pay the next time we ate out, Ben throws some bills on the table and ushers me out the door. We both know Belle Boutique is closing its doors, which means I'm out of a job. Again.

Ben drives to Erik Sinclair's place, and we knock on the front door. Going to a potential killer's house without police backup isn't the brightest idea I've ever had, but with Garrett in a hospital bed, I don't have an officer of the law on speed dial at the moment.

"If he gets suspicious, you run back to the truck," Ben says.

I'm about to tell him I'm not going to leave him to die when the front door opens.

Erik Sinclair's gaze falls on me. "You again?"

"Hi, Mr. Sinclair. I was just talking to Cynthia Lynch." I have no idea why I choose to lead with that information.

"Oh yeah? What's that got to do with me?"

"Well, she told us that you and Simone were supposed to sign a contract so she could sell your designs, but Simone backed out at the last minute. I was hoping you could tell us what happened."

"Why does it matter? Simone is dead."

"I know, but it seems like she had issues with some of her designers."

"And I wasn't one of them."

He's not going to offer up any information to us.

"Mr. Sinclair, you had the keycode to the back door of the boutique."

"Laurent gave it to me when we both thought I'd be working with Simone."

"Right. But when you came into the boutique on Monday, you used the front door."

"We're told to use the front door during regular business hours unless we're bringing a shipment of designs in."

"Did Simone have you bring in any designs?" I ask.

"No. I was supposed to come in on Sunday to sign the contracts and then deliver the designs on Monday, but Simone reneged on our deal on Sunday."

"And you came on Monday to get her to reconsider?" I ask.

"I decided to give her a chance to see she was making a big mistake by turning me away."

"But she refused to see you." Which made him angry. I witnessed that myself.

"You were there."

"Yes, I remember it well."

"What are you trying to get at anyway? I've already been questioned by the police. If they thought I was guilty of something, I wouldn't be standing here."

"Do you know about Detective Bilson's car accident yesterday?" I ask.

"I heard about it on the news. Is he going to make it?"

"Yes, he's expected to make a full recovery."

Erik bobs his head.

"Mr. Sinclair, how well do you know Cynthia Lynch?"

"I know she makes handbags. That's about it. I think we're done here." He's eager to get rid of us. He even starts to shut the door.

"You knew about the delivery from your company last Monday."

He pauses. "I don't work on Mondays."

"Exactly. And that's why you chose to kill Simone on a Monday. You knew Maxwell Decker would take the fall because he'd be there to deliver the package you knew was being delivered. You planned it all out. You wanted to make Simone pay for the way she toyed with you."

Erik opens the door fully, and Ben puts a protective arm out in front of me. "Tell me why you think you're qualified to solve a murder when you work in a boutique."

"Tell me why you murdered Simone over her not signing that contract with you. You could have taken your work elsewhere."

"You're new to town, right?" he asks me, like I'm a complete idiot. "Rockland has one high-end boutique. One. Simone was my only shot. I'm a deliveryman. Do you know what I make in a week?"

Probably more than I do.

Erik steps out onto the porch, forcing Ben and me to back away. "I can't afford to move to New York or Milan. I can't just drop everything and follow my dream. No. If I wanted something to happen for me, I had to make it happen."

"And that's why you killed Simone. She was standing between you and your dream," I say. "You probably thought with her out of the way, you could convince Laurent to sign that contract and sell your designs."

"You have two seconds to get out of my face before I get my gun."

"Are you threatening us?" I ask.

Ben pulls me toward the truck. "Hailey, get in."

"Get out of here!" Erik yells after us.

Ben and I get in the truck, and he pulls out of the driveway as fast as he can.

"He just threatened to use a gun on us," I say.

"I know. I'm going to the station. We need to report this to whoever took over the case for Detective Bilson."

The only other person I know at the Rockland PD is Officer Casey. He's young, only in his early thirties, and he seems nice enough. I look around the station for him.

"Can I help you?" a female officer asks me.

"Yes, I'm looking for Officer Casey. Is he here?"

"No, he's not. Can I help you?"

"Um, do you know who is handling the Simone Vincent case now that Detective Bilson is in the hospital?"

"That case is closed," she says.

"No, Detective Bilson was investigating the murder when he had his accident."

"I'm sorry, but you're mistaken. The man responsible for Simone Vincent's murder was already arrested." She means Maxwell Decker.

"Yes, I know the man who was discovered holding the murder weapon was initially charged with the murder, but Detective Bilson was pursuing a new lead in the case.

"I'm afraid I'm not aware of what it is you're referring to. As far as anyone here knows, the case is closed."

"What about Laurent Vincent? He was supposed to be evaluated by a psychologist the station hired."

"I'm afraid I'm not at liberty to discuss this with you, but I can assure you that we have the guilty party in custody. Do you work at the boutique? Is that why you're inquiring about the murder?"

"Yes, but—"

She holds up a hand to stop me. "I know rumors can spread through town like wildfire. And that Rumor Robin column is no help. But Rockland is a safe place to live. I see no reason why you should be afraid to go back to work at the boutique."

She's not going to listen to us. Without Garrett Bilson on the case, we're going to be completely on our own.

Since the police station was a dead end, Ben and I drive to the hospital to check on Garrett. Nurse Maggie comes over to us when she sees me.

"How's he doing?" I ask her.

"He's been in and out of consciousness all day."

"Has he said anything?" I ask.

"No, I'm afraid not. We still don't have any answers about what caused the accident or how badly Detective Bilson's brain was injured in the crash. Your friend has been in there with him the entire time. I had to bring her some food because she refuses to leave his side."

"Are we allowed in the room?" I ask.

Nurse Maggie looks around. "I sort of told the doctor that your friend Riley is the detective's fiancé. It was the only way I could get her access to the room. Why don't you let me tell her you're here and see if I can convince her to step out for a moment to talk to you?" She offers me a small smile, and I nod. She disappears inside the room. About forty seconds later, Riley comes out.

She looks like she's been crying for the better part of the day. "Hey." She wipes at her cheeks.

I give her a hug and bring her over to a group of chairs not far from Garrett's room. "How are you holding up?"

"He opened his eyes a few times. He didn't talk, though. Do you think he can't talk?"

"I don't know, but I actually asked how you're doing. Nurse Maggie filled me in on Garrett already."

"What did she tell you? I feel like she's keeping things from me because she doesn't think I can handle it. Did she say when they think he'll—"

"Riley, breathe. They don't really know much. We have to be patient and let Garrett recover at his own pace."

"I hate this. I'm so mad at him for doing this to me."

That's so typical Riley. "I'm sure he'll be himself again soon, and then you can let him have it for making you worry."

"I will, too."

"I have no doubt."

"How's the investigation going?" She looks at Ben now since he's been silent.

"Erik Sinclair seems like the most likely suspect. We're pretty convinced it's not Laurent," Ben says.

"Talk to Pete. He knows everyone. He might remember something about Erik Sinclair that can help you."

I nod. "We will. Hey, Pete was there to pull Garrett out of the car."

"Yeah, so?" Riley asks.

"Well, Nurse Maggie said that the police got conflicting accounts of the accident. I wonder if Pete saw it and knows what really happened."

"If anyone knows, it's most likely him," Riley says. She jerks a thumb over her shoulder. "I should get back in there. I don't want him to wake up and be alone." She gets to her feet.

"Go." I squeeze her hand before she walks back into the room.

"I take it we're going to Town Square to find Pete Modell," Ben says.

"Yeah, that seems like the most logical next step."

When we arrive in Town Square the crowd on the sidewalk is in an uproar. Ben and I walk over to the nearest group and ask them what's going on.

"It's the latest Rumor Robin column," a woman says. "It says Simone Vincent was planning to leave Rockland to pursue her own future as a fashion designer."

Oh no. Riley wrote another column from the hospital? I guess that was how she was filling the time while Garrett slept. She used all the information I've uncovered on the case and aired it for the public.

Ben grabs a copy of the paper from a man standing next to him, and we both read it. "The family is going to be insanely upset about this," he says.

"But this might be a good thing. The police are convinced the case is closed, but Rumor Robin may have given them a reason to reconsider." Now I understand. Riley is doing what she can to make sure this case gets solved for Garrett. She can't be out here with Ben and me searching for the killer, so she did the only thing she could think of to help us. She got people talking about the murder.

Ben and I listen as several people spout theories.

"I don't know why the police would ever have entertained the idea that it was the deliveryman to begin with. Like Rumor Robin says, he had no motive."

"Simone was trying to steal money from her own designers," a woman says. "I bet one of them killed her."

"I think it was her brother, Laurent. He probably found out Simone was going to leave him and take her contacts with her."

Ben hands the paper back to the man he borrowed it from, and we step away from the crowd.

"That Rumor Robin did Maxwell a huge favor," Pete says.

I turn around to face him. "We were looking for you," I tell him.

"I figured. You want to know if I saw the car accident, don't you?"

I nod. "There have been several eyewitness accounts, but none of the stories match."

"That's because it happened so fast."

"Can you tell us what you saw?" I ask him.

Pete nods. "Detective Bilson was coming up on the light, and he started yelling something about it being red. But the light was green. This woman was so confused. She was at the crosswalk, waiting to walk, and he was yelling, 'Red! It's red!' I think she assumed he was trying to tell her it was okay to cross because she started to walk, and he almost hit her. He swerved and hit the lamppost instead."

That doesn't make any sense. Why would he tell her the light was red if it wasn't?

CHAPTER NINETEEN

Pete cocks his head at me. "I know what you're thinking, Hailey, but that's what I saw."

"Do you know who the woman was?" I ask. I can't believe she didn't go to the police to tell them what happened.

Pete lowers his head. He doesn't want to tell us. There's only one woman I know Pete would go to great lengths to protect. Mia Emerson. He's in love with her. She's part of the reason Pete wound up doing community service for accidental manslaughter.

"It's okay, Pete. You don't have to say her name." I reach for his arm and gently squeeze it.

"How is Detective Bilson doing?" he asks.

"No change really."

"Tell Riley I said to hang in there. Garrett Bilson is tough."

"I'll tell her." I offer him a sympathetic smile since he's well aware we're going to talk to Mia next.

She works at the bakery in Town Square, so we walk there. I don't want to spook Mia, so Ben and I order coffee and two muffins. She brings them to our table in the corner.

"Nice to see you guys," she says, but I'm not sure she really means it since my only interactions with her have pertained to the death of her former boyfriend.

"Hi, Mia. I'm glad you're doing okay after the car accident." It's risky leading with that, but I want her to know we're aware of what happened.

She pulls out a chair at the table and sits down with us. "Did you see me?" she asks.

I'm not about to throw Pete under the bus, so I just nod. "Can you tell us what happened?"

She looks down at her apron. "I'm not even sure."

"Just do your best," Ben says in a sympathetic tone.

Mia bobs her head and takes a deep breath. "I was standing at the crosswalk, waiting for the light to change. I saw the patrol car coming, and Detective Bilson was yelling something about the light being red. But it wasn't. I checked."

"Why did you cross the road then?" I ask.

"Because he just kept yelling. I thought maybe the light was broken, and he was telling me to cross. He's a police officer, so I wasn't going to argue with him."

"That's when you crossed the road," I say.

"And he didn't slow down. I didn't know what to think. I started running to avoid being hit."

"Did you see him hit the lamppost?" I ask.

"No. I heard it. I was so shaken up by almost being hit, and I just kept running." She covers her face with her hands and sobs into them. "I know I should have stayed and talked to the police, but I was so scared. I don't understand what happened, and I felt so guilty. It's my fault he crashed."

I reach for her, placing my hand on her shoulder. "I don't think it was your fault. You did what you thought he was telling you to do."

"But the crosswalk sign told me not to cross, and I disobeyed it. No one was going to believe me if I said Detective Bilson told me to cross when I wasn't supposed to. He's an officer of the law."

I understand why she thinks that. I also know that Pete saw the whole thing and told Mia to run. He probably ran to her aid, which is why some people thought they saw a man running across the road. It was Pete, chasing after Mia and telling her to get out of there. He'd do anything to protect her. I don't tell Mia I know that because I'm pretty sure she'd deny it to protect Pete as well.

Pete probably feels responsible for his part, which is why he risked his life to pull Garrett from the car. He had to make up for telling Mia to get out of there.

"I need to tell the police what really happened, don't I?"

"Mia, we're not going to say anything. Whether or not you do is completely up to you."

"How is he doing?" she asks. "Do you know?"

"He's being monitored. He's been in and out of consciousness."

"But will he make it?" Her bottom lip trembles.

"The doctors expect him to, yes."

Relief washes over her features. She goes back to work, leaving Ben and me to eat our muffins.

"Why do you think Detective Bilson was saying the light was red?" Ben asks.

"We might have to wait to ask him when he wakes up." I have to wonder if Riley would know. Was it part of a memory they shared from their childhood? Garrett was upset when he left Riley's place, so maybe he was thinking about something from their past and yelling to himself about it in the car on the drive back to the station. It's possible he wasn't yelling to Mia at all. She only thought he was.

We finish our muffins, and I start toward the boutique.

"Whoa. What are you doing?" Ben asks, grabbing my arm to stop me.

"I'm going to turn in Leslie's resignation letter and her key. I don't want anything to do with the boutique."

"What about Maxwell Decker?" Ben asks. "If we give up on this case, he's going to go to jail for a murder he didn't commit."

"I don't know what else to do, Ben. I can't get the officers at the station to believe me about the murder. Without Garrett, we're stuck." I sigh. "Maybe Garrett will be able to find some evidence to reopen the case once he recovers. But for now, I'm done."

"Okay, I guess you're right, but Riley is not going to like this."

No, she's not. Especially after she wrote that Rumor Robin column to try to help us solve the case. I try listening to the crowd as we walk through it to the boutique.

"Erik Sinclair threw quite the fit when Simone sent him packing."

"Simone only cared about Ruby. She didn't need those other designers."

"Cynthia Lynch was bitter enough to kill her."

"Nah, if Cynthia did it, she would have beat her with one of her own handbags." A few people laugh at that, which makes me wonder how they can possibly see anything humorous about a murder. I'm choosing to think they're the type who laugh when they get scared, and they aren't really unfeeling people.

When we reach the boutique, it's closed. I knew it would be, so I slide the envelope with Leslie's resignation and key under the door. Now no one will know Ben and I ever used her key. I hate the feeling I get afterward, though.

I'm giving up.

I look at Ben with tears in my eyes. "I can't do it."

"I had a feeling you were going to say that." He wraps an arm around me. "What do you want to do."

"I want to talk to Laurent. He and Ivy are the only ones who saw what was on the flash drive. They know more than anyone."

"You're certain he didn't kill Simone?" Ben asks.

I nod. I may not care for Laurent anymore now that I know he was only pretending to be nice when we met, but I don't believe he killed anyone.

"Let's go then."

We drive to Laurent and Ivy Vincent's home. They're both there and more than a little surprised to see us.

"Hailey, I admit I didn't think I'd be seeing you anymore after our last encounter down at the police station," Laurent says. "Do you still think I murdered my sister?"

"No, I don't. I do think you and your lawyer faked that psych evaluation to get you off the hook, and I think you're a good actor who fooled a lot of people into believing Simone was the nasty sibling, but I don't think you're a killer."

He laughs. "Well, I guess that's something." He stops laughing. "You may consider yourself fired as well."

"Glad to hear it because that means I can collect unemployment until Ben finds me a new job placement." I smirk at him. "Anyway, I'm here because I think we can both agree Maxwell Decker didn't kill your sister. Someone else did. I'm guessing either Erik Sinclair or Cynthia Lynch."

"Cynthia Lynch wouldn't get her hands dirty for anyone. She's not capable of murder."

My money was on Sinclair anyway. "Fair enough. We heard Erik Sinclair had a public disagreement with Simone the day before she died."

"That's true."

"And it's why you met with him on Monday and wouldn't let him near Simone," I add.

He holds his hands out at his sides. "See. I was protecting my sister, even if I didn't know she didn't deserve it at the time."

"She screwed you over with the business."

"She tried to. Whoever killed her actually did me a favor."

"Laurent!" Ivy smacks his arm. "Don't go saying things like that. You make yourself sound guilty."

"Like I said, I don't believe either of you killed anyone." I wave my hand in the air. "Back to Sinclair. Do you think he could have used the keycode to let himself into the storage room?"

Laurent lowers his head.

"Wait. You did disable the chime on the back door. Why?"

"I'm not admitting to anything," he says.

"I have a video, which I've already given to the police," I add in case he gets any ideas of trying to abduct me or something crazy like that to keep me from sharing the evidence, "of you messing with the door to fix that alarm."

"I hated that stupid alarm. We have a keycode for a reason. No one can get in without it, so what was the sense of having an annoying blaring sound go off every time someone opened the door? I was always the one who heard it since my office was right next to the storage room."

"So you disabled it to give yourself some peace and quiet?" I ask.

He sighs. "That's not a crime."

No, it's not, but it helped the real killer commit a very big crime. "Did anyone know you disabled the chime?"

"At first, I thought maybe Simone and Ruby caught me doing it because they came into the storage room right after I disabled it, but neither said a word, so I suppose I got away with it."

Simone would have most likely laid into him if she did know because that was her personality. She wouldn't care that the chime bothered her brother. She probably barely heard it from her office, especially if her door was closed, which it usually was.

"I know you don't care who killed your sister, but can you really let an innocent man go to jail for a crime he didn't commit?" I ask.

"What do you want from me? The police have already suspected me, and I'm not interested in going down that path again."

I decide to appeal to his business sense. "Don't you think it would be better for you if the public saw you as the grieving brother who was determined to not only find his sister's killer but help an innocent man go free?"

He pauses and turns to Ivy.

She bobs her head. "It probably was Sinclair. He was angry enough with Simone, and getting him out of our hair will only be good for us."

"Okay, I'll go to the station and tell the police about Sinclair's fight with Simone and his knowledge of the back door code. Happy?" he asks me.

"Make sure you tell them you don't believe Maxwell Decker is guilty. Then I'll be happy."

Laurent closes the door in my face.

"Think he'll actually do it?" Ben asks.

"I hope so, but after he had that psych evaluation, I'm not sure they'll put much stock in what he has to say." His lawyer basically tried to make Laurent seem crazy because of grief. It's going to discredit any theories Laurent goes to the police with now. "I think maybe we should try to get Ruby on board with this plan, too. She was Simone's only friend. She might actually be willing to help us find the real killer."

"But we still don't know how to find her since the only address that came up was in New York City."

He's right. I can only think of one person who might know where she lives, other than Laurent, who I'm pretty sure wouldn't open his door to us again even if I had a suitcase of hundreds open and facing his peephole. He's had enough of me.

I call Riley.

"Hello?" she says. She sounds a little better.

"Riley, I'm so sorry to bother you, but I need a quick favor."

"What is it?"

"We need to find out where Ruby Redford lives."

"She lives in the cottage on Simone Vincent's property."

"You're kidding me." I knew they were close, but I had no idea Simone and Ruby were so close that they lived on the same property.

"Yeah. Why are you—wait. Garrett?" she asks. "Garrett, it's Riley. Can you hear me?"

"Is he waking up?"

"He's mumbling."

"What is he saying?"

"I don't know. I can't make it out. Hailey, I should go."

"Okay, I—" I stop talking when I realize the call's already ended.

"Is he awake?" Ben asks.

"She said he was trying to talk."

"That's a good sign, right?"

"I would think so."

"Did she know where Ruby lives?" he asks since he couldn't hear Riley's side of the conversation.

"Yeah, she lives on Simone Vincent's property."

"That means Laurent and Ivy were probably right about Simone and Ruby being in on this business plan together."

We jump back in the truck and drive to Vance Brook's house. Simone was plotting right underneath her husband's and brother's noses. And Ruby was helping her do it. What they did wasn't actually a crime, but I'm hoping the fact that they were as thick as thieves will make Ruby want to find Simone's killer.

The cottage on the property is actually so far away you'd never know it was the same property, but that's how much land the Vincent's own here. Ben parks in front of it, and we knock on the door.

Ruby answers, wearing her hair in a messy bun with several charcoal pencils sticking out of it. "Can I help you?"

"Ruby, we need to talk to you about Simone."

"What about her?"

"We know you two were close. Laurent found Simone's future business plans. You two were going to split off on your own and leave him behind." I figure it's best to lay it all out there at once.

"So? Is he threatening to come after me or something?"

"No, nothing like that." At least, he didn't mention it to me, not that he would. He fired me.

"Then why are you here? You work at the boutique, right?"

"Not anymore. We're trying to find out who really killed Simone. We know it wasn't the deliveryman, and seeing as you were Simone's only real friend, we thought you might want to help us get to the bottom of this."

She lowers her head. "Come in." She steps aside to let us in. "Can I get you something to drink?"

"No, but could I use your bathroom?" Ben asks. "We drank a lot of coffee."

She points down a hallway. "Second door on the right."

"Thank you." Ben looks at me. "Be right back."

I follow Ruby into the kitchen.

"Have a seat." She turns on her heel. "I forgot to tell him that doorknob sticks. I'll be right back." She disappears down the hallway, and I sit down at the table.

There's a design book lying open, and I notice the designs are very different than what Ruby sells in the boutique. These are bolder. Riskier designs. I flip through a few pages before closing the book. On the cover is one word. Red.

"It's red," I say, repeating what Mia and Pete told us Garrett Bilson was yelling before the car crash.

"How did you figure it out?" Ruby asks, walking back into the room, holding a gun.

CHAPTER TWENTY

I stare at the gun in Ruby's hand. This can't be right. "No. You were with Jesse in Simone's office when she was killed."

She smiles. "It was that detective, wasn't it? He found the voice mails on Simone's phone."

What messages? I have no idea what she's talking about. Did Garrett recover some voice mails that led him to identifying the killer? Is that what he was doing on the drive to the station? I can see how that would distract him from the road. And if he realized that Ruby was the killer and was referring to the Red clothing line while driving, that's what Mia heard. She thought he was talking about the traffic light, but he meant the clothing line.

"Red was Simone's line, wasn't it? The line she was putting out under your name."

Ruby scoffs. "It was dreadful. I hated being associated with that garbage." Ruby didn't want to let Simone use her name? I thought they were in on this together, but did Ruby grow tired of the arrangement?

"But you were with Jesse. You have an alibi."

"Of course, I do. I made sure of it."

She planned this. "You came in at the end of the day on purpose because you knew that's when Leslie counts the drawer. You did see Laurent deactivate the chime on the storage room door, but you kept that information from Simone because you knew it meant you'd be able to sneak in and kill Simone later. And then when you heard the chime of the register, you told Jesse it was the back door chime because it gave you a plausible reason for Simone to be out of her office when you got there."

"Very good, Hailey. You've figured it all out."

Not all of it. I still don't know how all of this happened. Everyone was convinced Simone and Ruby were good friends. Even Simone thought they were. "I don't understand. She was letting you showcase your own designs as well as hers, and you got to take public credit for all of them."

"Stupid girl. None of those designs were mine. Not a single one! She wouldn't let me use anything I came up with myself. Both lines were hers. Ruby was her classic line, and Red was her more risky stuff she wasn't sure would sell as well. The only money I made was peanuts for letting her use my fake name and for me to play the part when she needed a face behind the name."

"But you must have agreed to this deal to begin with," I say.

She gives one short, loud laugh. "Agreed? More like she coerced me into it. She caught me stealing one of her designs a while back." She waves a hand in the air. "It wasn't even that good, but I copied it because I was in a terrible slump. Simone threatened to expose me for the theft unless I agreed to her plan. What choice did I have? She would have ruined my reputation."

It doesn't sound like Ruby even had a reputation yet back then. Simone made her a star in the fashion world, but it was on Simone's terms. "Jesse said you spoke highly of Simone."

"Of course, I did. Especially to him. He's a talker. I needed everyone to think we were great friends. Even Simone thought so by the end."

She knew Jesse would tell everyone how much Ruby adored Simone. Ruby used Jesse to make everyone think she had this great relationship with Simone and get any and all suspicion off her.

"You showed up on Monday, and Simone thought you were there to talk about work, didn't she?"

"She sent me new designs. These dreadful things she wanted me to create. I couldn't do it. I'd had enough."

"But you didn't even tell her that, did you?" They didn't fight. Laurent would have heard them if they had. No, Ruby pretended everything was fine, and then bashed Simone's skull in with the clothing rack once her back was turned.

"There's no reasoning with Simone Vincent. She only cared about herself. Her ideas. Her plans. No one else mattered. I watched her steal from the other designers. She lied to every single one of them, pocketing their money so she could save up for her move to New York."

"She was taking you with her, though."

"You make it sound like she gave me a choice. I didn't have a choice. She told me what I was going to do. She even made me live here on her property so she could keep an eye on me." Her face is bright red now.

I hear Ben banging on the bathroom door. "Did you lock him in there?" I ask.

She bobs one shoulder. "The doorknob sticks."

I don't believe that for a second. She locked him in there because she thought we knew the truth about her when we got here. She probably thought us splitting up was part of a plan we came up with to trap her.

We do need a plan. I can't get to my phone with her gun aimed at me. She'd never allow it. My only hope is that Ben has called the station. Maybe I can scare Ruby into turning her back on me by yelling to him. "Ben, call the police. She has a gun!"

"Shut your mouth," she says, and she fires the gun.

I fall to the floor even though she misses. Thankfully, she's an awful shot. I duck under the table for cover.

Ben is screaming and banging on the bathroom door now. I hear wood splinter, and then Ruby screams. The gun goes off again and then slides across the floor to me. I don't want to touch it, but I don't want her to get it again either, so I kick it away.

When I scramble out from under the table, Ben has Ruby facedown on the floor and is sitting on top of her.

"Are you okay?" he asks me. "When I heard the gun go off…" He can't finish his sentence.

"I'm okay. Tell me you called the police."

"I did. The call's still connected." He looks behind him at his phone on the floor.

I run over to pick it up. "Hello?"

"Ma'am, are you all right? I heard gun shots," the woman says, and I recognize the voice as the woman we spoke to at the station.

"Yes. Ruby Redford just tried to kill me, but we have her apprehended. Please send help. We're at her home on Simone Vincent's property."

"I have Officer Casey en route to you now. Please stay on the line with me until he gets there."

"She admitted to killing Simone Vincent," I say.

The female officer gets quiet for a moment. "I'll be happy to take your full statement once Officer Casey brings Ms. Redford to the station."

I'm pretty sure that's the closest I'm going to get to an apology from her.

Nurse Maggie sneaks Ben and me into Garrett's room. "He's awake," she tells us. "And he's asking for you."

"He doesn't have amnesia?" I ask.

"No, he doesn't." She smiles at us and opens the door to his room.

As soon as she sees us, Riley jumps up to hug me. "How did you figure it out?"

"I didn't." I let go of her and look at Garrett. "But you did. That's what you were saying when the accident happened."

He gives me a faint smile. "I was listening to Simone's voice mails. I could tell Ruby was hiding something. Her tone didn't match her words. I don't know how Simone didn't pick up on it, but it all made sense to me."

"How did she kill Simone and get herself an alibi?" Riley asks.

"She killed Simone and then immediately came in to see her for a meeting," I say.

"What kind of psychopath can kill a person and then appear completely normal seconds later?" she asks.

"I think you just answered your own question." She was a psychopath. Plain and simple.

"I'm glad to see you're okay," I tell Garrett.

"Is Mia Emerson all right? That's who I almost hit, right?" he asks.

I nod. "She hasn't told the police it was her."

Garrett sighs. "Then maybe I don't remember that."

"What? Why would you do that?" Riley asks.

"Because I arrested Pete Modell's friend. From what I hear, Pete is the reason I'm alive right now. I think I can repay him by not mentioning the woman he's in love with was the woman I almost hit. From what I've pieced together, the accident was my fault anyway." He looks at me. "She thought I was telling her the light was red, didn't she?"

I nod.

"Thank you both for not giving up on the case," Garrett says.

"Riley wouldn't let us," I say. "Neither would Rumor Robin. She wrote about all the shady business going on with the family and the designers. She got the town talking and the police open to the idea that they might have the wrong man in custody."

"I'll have to thank her," Garrett says.

"You actually know who Rumor Robin is?" Ben asks.

Garrett smiles. "She's my hero."

"Come on," I say to Ben. "Detective Bilson needs his rest."

"I'm off duty. Call me Garrett," he says.

"Feel better soon," I tell him before backing out of the room.

I close the door over but don't click it shut.

Ben furrows his brow at me, but I hold a finger up to my lips and peek through the small opening in the door.

"So your head feels okay?" Riley asks.

"No, it hurts like crazy," Garrett says. "But my memory seems to be intact."

"Then you remember you were mad at me?"

"Are you prepared to pick another fight with me if I do?" he jokes. "It seems to be our thing."

"It's just that the doctors weren't sure you'd remember who you were, so I thought…" She pauses. "I thought maybe you wouldn't remember me," she says in a small voice.

Garrett gently places his hand on top of hers. "I couldn't never forget you, Riles. Never."

I close the door and smile at Ben. "I think they're going to be okay."

"How about us?"

"Were we fighting, and I somehow didn't know about it?" I ask, not sure why he'd ask that.

He smiles. "No, but I am confused about something."

"What's that?" We walk toward the elevators, and I stop to face him as we wait.

"This." He motions between us. "You and me."

"Are you asking what we are?"

"Is it too soon to ask that?"

"I don't think anyone in town would think so. Leslie even referred to you as my man."

"And you didn't correct her?" he asks.

"How could I when she wasn't wrong?" I smile up at him.

He leans down to kiss me as the elevator arrives. He drapes an arm across my shoulders and leads me into the elevator. "Good, then I'm taking my girlfriend to dinner to celebrate."

"I approve of that plan. And at dinner we can discuss where you think you might be able to find me a new job."

"How about we leave that to tomorrow? We deserve an evening off from work and murder investigations."

"I couldn't agree more."

If you enjoyed the book, please consider leaving a review. And look for the next book in the Traumatic Temp Agency series *Poisoning at the Pizzeria*.

ALSO BY KELLY HASHWAY

Traumatic Temp Agency Series:
Corpse at the Candy Shop
Tragedy at the Toy Shop
Bludgeoning at the Boutique

Piper Ashwell Psychic P.I. Series:
A Sight For Psychic Eyes
A Vision A Day Keeps the Killer Away
Read Between the Crimes
Drastic Crimes Call for Drastic Insights
You Can't Judge a Crime by its Aura
Fortune Favors the Felon
Murder is a Premonition Best Served Cold
It's Beginning to Look a Lot Like Murder
A Jailbird in the Vision is Worth Two in the Prison
Great Crimes Read Alike
I Spy With My Psychic Eye Someone Dead
A Vision in Time Saves Nine
There's No Crime Like the Prescient
Fight Fire With Foresight
Something Old, Something New, Something Foretold, Corpse So Blue

Murder Is In the Eye of the Beholder
Between a Vision and a Hard Case
THere's More Than One Way to Sense a Killer

Cup of Jo Mysteries:
Coffee and Crime
Macchiatos and Murder
Cappuccinos and Corpses
Frappes and Fatalities
Lattes and Lynching
Glaces and Graves
Espresso and Evidence
Americanos and Assault
Doppios and Death
Ristretto and Revenge
Viennas and Vendettas

Holidays Can Be Murder:
Valentine Victim
Fourth of July Fatality

Madison Kramer Mysteries:
Manuscripts and Murder
Sequels and Serial Killers
Fiction and Felonies

ACKNOWLEDGMENTS

Many thanks to Patricia Bradley for your editorial skills. Your feedback is greatly appreciated. To my VIP reader group and ARC team, thank you for your support. To my family and friends, thank you for not getting tired of me talking about my books. And to my readers, thank you for allowing me to share my characters with you.

ABOUT THE AUTHOR

Kelly Hashway fully admits to being one of the most accident-prone people on the planet, but luckily, she gets to write about female sleuths who are much more coordinated than she is. Maybe it was growing up watching *Murder, She Wrote* that instilled a love of mystery, but she spends her days writing cozy mysteries. Kelly's also a sucker for first love, which is why she writes romance under the pen name Ashelyn Drake. When she's not writing, Kelly works as an editor and also as Mom, which she believes is a job title that deserves to be capitalized.